Hermann Bokum

Wanderings

North and South

Hermann Bokum

Wanderings
North and South

ISBN/EAN: 9783337195939

Printed in Europe, USA, Canada, Australia, Japan

Cover: Foto ©Andreas Hilbeck / pixelio.de

More available books at **www.hansebooks.com**

WANDERINGS NORTH AND SOUTH,

BY

HERMANN BOKUM,

CHAPLAIN, U. S. A.,

TURNER'S LANE HOSPITAL.

————◄•◉•►————

PHILADELPHIA:
KING & BAIRD, PRINTERS, No. 607 SANSOM STREET,
1864.

PREFACE.

The "Testimony of a Refugee from East Tennessee," being the first of the four articles contained in this little volume, was published more than two years ago, and shortly after my having left the, so-called, Confederate States. Having revisited East Tennessee in the course of this year, the changes I met with and the change which in many respects had taken place in my own views, has given rise to the second article, "Sketches of East Tennessee Life." The third article, "Life and Death of a Christian Soldier," which appeared some time ago in the *Episcopal Recorder*, exhibits a combination of christian faithfulness and self-sacrificing loyalty. The reappearance of it will be welcomed, I know, by many. The last article, "The Turner's Lane Hospital," bears marks of the haste with which it has been prepared. Our time is a time for deeds, rather than for the recording of deeds. From my intimacy with some of the hospital chaplains, I know that this is the cause of their silence. *The Turner's Lane Hospital*, is a small one, in comparison with some others; it can accommodate only about three hundred patients; still what I have said about it will prove I trust not altogether void of instruction as well as interest.

HERMANN BOKUM.

Turner's Lane Hospital.
Philadelphia, Dec. 22d, 1864.

(iii)

A REFUGEE'S TESTIMONY.

(1)

A REFUGEE'S TESTIMONY.

It may seem bold and self-confident, indeed, that in the face of the multitude of pamphlets, addresses, essays and treatises, which this war has called forth, I should add one or more to the number. And yet there are some facts connected with my past history and my present position, which may sufficiently account for my appearing before the public just at this time. Born and educated in Germany, I arrived in this country in my twenty-first year, and after having spent twenty-eight years in the North, under circumstances which were especially calculated to endear to me the historic life, and the institutions of the country I had adopted, I lived in East Tennessee till treason there overthrew, for a time at least, the Government of the United States. My attachment to the Union compelled me to leave my home and my family to avoid a dungeon. It was then, when for more than a year I had had to witness the effects of a military despotism, which exalted falsehood, fraud and robbery to the rank of virtues, and rode rough-shod over every one that was unwilling to adopt this creed, that I prayed God that the time might come when I, in some humble way, might bear witness to the fearfulness of the crime, which, by means the most foul, had in that region of country at least, placed at the mercy of villains, the most abandoned, the noble and devoted men of the country. Similar prayers have risen from other lips, but their testimony will only be heard in the day of judgment, for they have sealed their faithfulness with their death. Yet it is not only recollections like these which now impel me to write. When after having fled from my home I at last had reached the lines of our troops which were then stationed near Cumberland Gap, I saw myself surrounded by hundreds of men with whom for years I had mingled at their altars and their firesides, and who like myself had been compelled to leave their homes and families. Impressed with the fact, that my past life would give me an influence in the North, which they could not have, they asked me to do all in my power to induce the men of the North to come to their relief, that they might be enabled with their swords to make their way back to their homes. I promised it, and now while I am about to fulfil this promise, I pray God that He may prepare for my words a ready access to the hearts of my readers. To all this I may add that I am once more standing upon the ground on which first I stepped when I came to this country, that not a few of those with whom I became acquainted in early life are now, when far advanced in years my honored friends, and that they have expressed a conviction that my extensive acquaintance in Pennsylvania, where for years I have labored as a preacher and a teacher, might enable me to impart information concerning the first workings and the gradual progress of treason in the South. Right or wrong I have acceded to their request, and I would have acceded sooner if my duties as chaplain of a hospital had not been of such a character as to claim the whole of my time.

East Tennessee, which late events have brought into such general notice, is a portion of that elevated region of country which embraces Southern Kentucky, Northern Alabama, Northern Georgia and Western North Carolina. The Cumberland Mountains in East Tennessee reach occasionally the height of 2,000 feet, they are rich in minerals, from their sides leap innumerable springs, flowing through productive valleys and emptying finally into the Tennessee or Cumberland rivers, the climate is magnificent, the scenery grand and picturesque, the population of an agricultural character, having comparatively few slaves. To this region of country I had moved in 1855, I had purchased a farm, planted vineyards and had gathered a small congregation. I had indulged the hope that in the same measure as I was endeavoring to make this home beautiful and productive, my children would resist the temptation to change, and this farm would be an heirloom in my family for many years to come. Beyond my spiritual sphere and these agricultural labors my ambition did not extend and with but a trifling change I could adopt with regard to myself and my family the beautiful lines of Barry Cornwall:

Touch us gently, Time!
Let us glide adown thy stream,
Gently as we sometimes glide
Through a quiet dream.

Humble voyagers are we,
Husband, wife and children three—
Two are lost—two angels fled
To the azure overhead.

These humble hopes, however, were not to be realized. It is now two years ago when I no longer could resist the conviction that we were standing on the very threshold of a treasonable attempt to break up the Union. At that time I happened to be in the house of one of my neighbors. In the course of the conversation the Union was mentioned by me. "The Union," said he, with a contemptuous smile, "the Union is gone!" I could hardly trust my ears. Here stood a man before me, who was not like myself an adopted citizen, but a native of this country, yet who was ready to obliterate from the family of nations the land which for more than thirty years I had learnt to regard as my own, and which had conferred on me innumerable blessings. "Hear me," said I to him, there was a time when the disciples of the Lord had called blessings upon Him;—the Pharisees asked him to stop his disciples, but the Lord told them that if his disciples were to be silent, the very stones would cry out. "You," added I, "were born in this country, you have Washington and his time handed down to you as a direct inheritance, I am but an adopted citizen, I am but as one of the stones, but as one of the stones I cry out against you." It was at that time that a great Union meeting was held in the vicinity of Knoxville. Horace Maynard was occupied in another part of the State, but Andrew Johnson and other leading Union men were there, and the question was seriously debated whether East Tennessee should take up arms and destroy the bridges in order to prevent the sending of rebel troops from Louisiana, Mississippi and Alabama to Virginia. Less extreme measures prevailed, the bridges were not burnt, the troops from the Southern States rushed into East Tennessee, and the Union men of East Tennessee were singly overpowered and disarmed. In the meantime Fort Sumter had fallen and some of the secessionists came to me and asked me to join the Southern Confederacy. "You remind me," said I, "of a good old bishop, when he was led to the stake he was advised to abjure the Savior and save his life. "Eighty and five years, was the answer of the bishop, has my Savior graciously protected me, and should I now forswear him?' So say I to you; thirty and five years has the flag of the Union with the help of God nobly protected me, and should I now forswear it?" The secessionists, however, became so violent in their measures that I found it necessary to go to Wash-ington in order to consult the Hon. Andrew Johnson, who by that time had succeeded in taking his place in Congress, and to find out whether we soon would obtain help or whether I would be compelled to move with my family to the North. When I went to Washington, Tennessee was still in the Union, when I returned it had been taken out by force and by fraud, and I was compelled to find my way through the Cumberland Mountains as best I might. Governor Harris had in vain endeavored to get a convention sanctioned by the people, by the means of which he had hoped to carry the State out of the Union. He had then called an extra session of the Legislature, and that body in violation of the express will of the people had declared an ordinance of separation on the 6th of May, submitting the question of Separation from the Federal Government and of Representation in the Richmond Congress to be voted on by the people on the 8th day of June. *Against* Separation from the Federal Government and Representation in Richmond, East Tennessee gave a majority of 18,300. It would have been much larger if the votes of rebel troops had not been counted, though under the constitution they had no authority to vote at any election. In this way however the State was forced out of the Union when a majority of her people were utterly averse to any such separation.

Having arrived at home after having past through many trying scenes, I found that my journey to the North had excited attention, and that threats had been made of hanging me as soon as I should return. I, however, had to visit Knoxville. When I entered the court house in that city, I found Judge Humphreys occupied in judging men, who had committed no crime, but in various ways had expressed their partiality for the Union. This is the same Judge Humphreys against whom others as well as myself were cited to bear testimony in Washington a few months ago, and who in consequence of that testimony was deposed from his office. When I had left the court house a friend took me aside, himself a secessionist, and told me that I would do well to leave the city, since in case the soldiers were to learn that I had just come from the North, I in a few minutes might be a dead man. Then came a time of darkness and oppression. The battle of Manassas had taken place, and for four months we were kept in the dark with regard to almost everything, which could have a favorable bearing on the preservation or restoration of the Union. It was during this time that Judge Humphreys held court again in Knoxville, and that he himself told the State's Attorney that he had no right to send Union men to Tuscaloosa unless they were taken with arms in their hands. The State's Attorney, a wretched drunkard, replied that they had only been sent to Tuscaloosa in order to make of them good Southern men. Shortly before this time some of the Union men had secretly combined and had burned certain bridges, in order to put a stop to the thousands of soldiers who were every day passing on to Virginia. Mr. Pickens who is now a Major in the U. S. Army, had taken part in this enterprise and had escaped. In consequence of it, his father, a Senator in the State's Legislature, had been seized and taken to Tuscaloosa. One of my neighbors returned at that time from Tuscaloosa, where he had been imprisoned, sick in body and in mind. He told me that he had left the aged Pickens in good health, but that he could not live, since he was confined with twenty-seven others in a small room, and in the night they were not permitted to open the windows. Pickens died. His wife when she heard it, lost her reason and died; a daughter being thus suddenly deprived of her parents also died of a broken heart! It was in this way that the State's Attorney in Knoxville made of Union men *Good Southern Men!* An acquaintance of mine, the Rev. Mr. Duggan, a highly respectable clergyman, was compelled on a hot day to walk twenty miles as a prisoner to Knoxville, because long before the State had been carried out of the Union he had prayed for the President of the United States. His horse was led behind him, and he, though old and very corpulent, was not permitted to mount it. When he had arrived in Knoxville, he was declared free, and free he soon was, for God took him to himself. That journey on foot had become the cause of his death. A man named Haun had been taken to prison, because he had taken part in the burning of the bridges. The names of the persons who tried him have never been made public. Not until he had arrived at the place of execution did the public learn why he was to be executed. He was asked whether he was sorry for what he had done, he replied, that if placed in similar circumstances he would do it again, and that he was prepared to die. Others beside him were hung, still others were shot down or otherwise murdered. Nor did this spirit of 'oppression extend to Union men alone. Shortly before I left East Tennessee, a wealthy secessionist named Jarnagan, who lived in my vicinity did not rest, till two companies were quartered in that town, in order to keep down the Union men. Three months afterwards he left his residence, because, as he himself declared, his own friends had robbed him of property worth $3,000, and would take his life if he would not give up all. It was still worse with Daniel Yarnall, another secessionist, and also one of my neighbors. He had complained concerning the conduct of some soldiers in the Confederate army, and these soldiers had been punished; in consequence of it they went to his house and stripped him. He himself counted forty lashes, and then could count no more. When the workings of this treason first commenced, and I on my missionary tours was passing through the fruitful valleys and over the pleasant hill sides of East Tennessee, and beheld the fields ready for the harvests, and the industrious men and women engaged in their daily round of duties, I asked myself, whether indeed it was possible, that the mad ambition of men would go so far as to desolate these scenes of beauty. It has proved possible indeed! Where but two years ago there were all the elements calculated to make a community prosperous, there is now misery and wretchedness the most fearful, and the rule of an armed mob bent upon indiscriminate plunder. Do you see yonder wretch? He has been a drunkard and a vagabond all his life-time, yet he has thousands of dollars in his pocket now, and he rides the most beautiful horse in that whole region of country. I could take you to the industrious farmer from whom he took the horse, and whom he robbed of his money, and who now, together with his wife and children are left in penury! Do you see yonder girl? How beautiful she would be, if it were not for the loss of that eye! That eye she lost in successfully defending her honor against the assault of a Confederate soldier, until her father could come to her aid and slay him. Ah, my reader, you who live here so comfortable and so undisturbed, have little knowledge of what is going on but a few hundred miles from here. I have seen the man of eighty, the oldest and the wealthiest man of a loyal district, who at his age had joined the Home Guards, raise his trembling hands to heaven, and ask God whether there was no curse in store for deeds so cruel. I have heard the gentle woman exclaim that she must have the blood of one of these men, her spirit being maddened to desperation because they had fired a hundred shots at her husband. Who could remain cold at the sight of enormities like these? I have often been asked whether the representations made by Brownlow and others can be relied on. Neither Brownlow nor myself, nor any, nor all of us can give a full record of cruelties which have been perpetrated and are now being perpetrated in the recesses of the mountains and valleys of East Tennessee, or of the sufferings and the deaths through which East Tennesseeans have to pass in the prisons of the South from want of food, from filth, from absence of ventilation and from degrading work.

After the defeat of the rebels near Mill Spring had taken place, I had to go secretly to Kentucky in order to attend to some private affairs of mine. After my return the battle of Pittsburg Landing had occurred, and Fort Henry, Fort Donelson and Nashville had fallen into the hands of the Federal troops. In consequence of these reverses the conscription law was enacted. There was a place of mustering near my house, where in former times generally some 800 men had mustered; that day only about 50 appeared. Two nights after, almost all the men able to bear arms disappeared, went to Kentucky, and entered the United States Army. Then Churchwell, the Provost Marshal of East Tennessee, a man who has since been called to the Judgment bar of God, issued a proclamation and declared that if these men would come back they should be permitted peacefully to pursue their avocations; at the same time, however, he attempted to seize some of the most influential Union men who had yet staid behind. I was to be one of the victims; by a most Providential combination of circumstances I received early notice of the fact that five men were sent out to apprehend me. I had made up my mind to go to prison. I could not bear the thought of leaving the atmosphere where my wife and my children were breathing, but my wife prevailed on me to go to our friends in the North. Her last words were: " Fear not for me, I trust in God;" I begged her to kiss our children, and I turned into the mountains. Never I trust, shall I cease to be thankful for the gracious manner in which I was shielded from harm in that perilous journey. Six months later my wife and my children arrived in Cincinnati, having crossed the Cumberland Mountains in the rear of the two contending armies, and having made more than 300 miles in an open buggy. We have since removed to this city, where I have been appointed Chaplain of the Turner's Lane Hospital.

Now, after having made these statements, which in a great measure refer to myself, I wish to draw the attention of the reader to certain subjects which are of vital importance to all of us, and on which my past experience, such as I have just described it, may enable me to shed some light. In the first place, then, let me advise every one who reads these pages to turn away from the man, who attempts to persuade himself and others, that the South has been driven into her treasonable course in consequence of the wrong inflicted on her by the North. This, indeed, is one of the falsehoods by

which the men of the South have attempted to excuse their
treason, but it was not the cause of it. Do you think, I
believed them, when they came to me about that time and
told me that the men of the North were a set of cowards
who would not fight, and that one Southerner could whip
five of them at any time? Do you think I believed them
when they spoke of drawing the line between the North and
the South along the Ohio river, and of erecting an immense
fortress opposite Cincinnati, and of battering down that city,
whenever the North interfered with slavery? Or do you
think I believed them, when they advised me to join the
South, because, if the South succeeded, East Tennessee would
be a great manufacturing country, and my little property
would increase a hundred-fold in value? Of course I did
not believe them. I knew too much about my friends in
the North to doubt their bravery, and I had seen too much
of the want of manufacturing enterprize in the South to
indulge the hope that my property would be worth any
thing, if the South should gain the ascendency. Just as
little did I believe it, when they came to me and told me
that they were compelled to rise in rebellion, because the
North was resolved to rob the South of their slaves. Had
not I listened to the Rev. Dr. Ross and many of the other
leaders of the movement? Washington and Jefferson and
the men of *their* time had, indeed, regarded slavery as an
evil which would gradually give way under the influence
of christianity; but not so these apostles of our own time
or of the immediate past. According to them, slavery is
the very foundation, on which christianity is resting, take it
away and christianity crumbles to pieces; according to them
on the existence of slavery depends the cause of freedom,
touch that institution and freedom as well as christianity
are crushed. Strange doctrines these, you say, yet these
are the doctrines which have been taught in the South by
divine and layman for more than twenty-five years, and
taught for the very purpose, which they now attempt to
realize by their treasonable movement, and into which they
have been drawn for reasons very different from those which
they have made public. It was indeed not abolition nor

any other imaginary wrong inflicted on them by the North,
which influenced their action, but a conviction of a very
different character. With all their boasts concerning the
divine character of the institution of slavery, and the spiritual and temporal blessings which resulted from it, they could
not conceal from themselves, that in its practical workings
slavery in many respects looked very much *like a curse*.
Why was it that these vast multitudes of emigrants were
peopling the North, while they kept away from the South?
Why, that manufactures and commerce selected the North
for their favored home? How did it happen that if you
started from Pittsburg on your way to St. Louis, you would
see on the right hand side of the Ohio river, flourishing
towns and cultivated fields without number, while on the
left, nature reigned beautiful but unproductive? It was
slavery which was the cause of it, and the time was fast
approaching when the South compared to the North would
be in a lamentable minority, and would lose that influence
over the General Government which it had so long enjoyed.
Hence the criminal resolve of breaking the Union to pieces,
and of founding an aristocratic empire with slavery for its
basis, and the prospect of having untold wealth, pouring
into its bosom by re-opening the African slave trade. Ah
what anguish have we Union men of the South suffered
when one and another of these diabolical plans was developed to our view. How vain the hope of being benefitted
by the resolutions of Crittenden, or by any other resolutions,
when we had learnt that the Union was to be broken to
pieces at every cost. Many an appeal reached the South at
that time from the great conservative body of the people in
the North, calling upon them to be but patient for a few
days and they should receive every security for their rights
which they possibly could desire. There were many hearts,
which bounded with joy and with hope at these appeals,
but they met no response in those Southern Senators, who
had it in their power to pass the Crittenden resolutions, but
who refused to vote, that they might break up the Union.
Abolition no doubt has to answer for many things, but it
never will have to answer for having brought about this

rebellion. The power was rapidly escaping from the hands which had wielded it so long, and that power was to be preserved, though the country should be deluged in blood, and the recollections of a glorious past be given to the winds. Yet there are still those amongst us, who are sympathizing with the South, on account of the wrongs it has suffered at the hands of the North. I assure you that the slaveholders of East Tennessee, who are Union men, do not feel that they need such sympathy. They never have complained that they have lost any of their rights, and they look with utter abhorrence upon this attempt to obliterate from the family of nations, a country which surpassed every other in a spirit of justice and humanity. They are most decidedly of opinion that God would be altogether just, if He should sweep away the institution of slavery, which these men intend to make the foundation of their empire, and if they also in consequence of it have to suffer loss they are prepared for it. It is by the preservation of the Union alone, that they can have security not only for the property which may be left them, but for liberty and life. Shortly before I left East Tennessee, I was in the house of a wealthy slave owner, a devoted friend of the Union. He spoke with tears of this attempt to break up the Union, adding that there was a report that the Government of the United States intended to confiscate the slaves. He did not believe, he said, that the Government would deprive loyal slaveholders of their property, but in case it should be necessary, in order to preserve the Union, he would gladly give up the slaves. Another slaveholder, also one of my acquaintances, who had been robbed of a large portion of his property, and who had been in prison for months, at last reached his home again. "The last dollar," he said to his wife, "the last slave, if but the Union be preserved, and joyfully we will start anew in life." "Think you," said another distinguished slaveholder, a refugee from East Tennessee,* the other day in the city of New York, in the same spirit, "that for the pleasure of enjoying the company of my wife and my babes whom I have not seen for the last two years, I would not have willingly given all

* The Rev. Mr. Carter.

that my negroes are worth, or all that they ever will be worth to me?" Yet though the Union men of the South thank them so little for their sympathy, the sympathizers here are still going on in the same strain. "Pray, sir," said one of them to me but a few days ago, how would you like it, if you had owned two hundred negroes and they had been taken away from you?" "1 would certainly feel satisfied," was my reply, "if at that price I had obtained security for the property I might still have, but most of all for my liberty and my life. I have not lost two hunderd slaves, but I have lost all the property I owned, and which I valued at six thousand dollars. Yet by giving it up and escaping to the North, I again enjoy the benefits resulting from the Union, and the means of supporting my family."

By facts like these I am readily reminded of others, which it may be as well to mention in this connection. I have very frequently heard of late the assertion, that this is not a war for the Union but for the freeing of the negroes, and gentlemen have told me, that they, indeed, are as much for the Union as ever, but that they are constrained to oppose the administration, because it has now raised issues which are altogether foreign to the original objects of the war. Now in order to meet this objection in a satisfactory manner, I beg the reader to look at the beginning of this war. When the South was going on in taking one aggressive step after the other, and the United States Government still bore it patiently, a gentleman, who is now prominent in the ranks of secession, but who at that time had not made up his mind which way he would turn, expressed great astonishment at this conduct. "The United States," he said, "are a powerful nation, but even for a nation so powerful it seems strange to be so slow in punishing treason." Ignorant as I then was of the extent of this treason, I gloried in this forbearance of the United States because it was so much in keeping with the spirit it had ever manifested to leave room for the loyalty that might still exist in the South to make itself felt. At a later period, however, the necessity of an energetic movement had become evident, and government and people unanimously declared that they were fighting, and would fight

on for the Union and the Constitution. I became well
acquainted with this state of feeling, for I was then in the
North. But then, again, there came another phase of the
struggle. The Federal arms had been sufficiently successful
in taking possession of large portions of slave territory, and
they had to meet the question, what they should do with
the negroes of disloyal slaveholders. The question was
finally solved by the proclamation of the President, a docu-
ment, which is the result of the circumstances in which the
disloyalists of the South have placed themselves by their
treasonable course. Thus it has happened that thousands,
and let me add, I am of the number, while they have at all
times opposed abolitionism, and have been in favor of securing the South in all their rights, have now come to feel, that
treason has no rights whatever, and that the negroes, if they
furnish to traitors the means of support, and of carrying on
this war against the Union, should be deprived of these
means wherever an opportunity offers, and that they ought
to sustain the Government to the utmost in their power,
because it is acting in accordance with these views. To
illustrate this subject from what may be called the common
sense view of it, I beg leave to relate an incident related
to me by a clergyman, whose name I shall be happy to give,
as soon as he will permit me to do so. He had been invited
to deliver a patriotic address in a neighborhood, which was
not celebrated on account of its patriotism, and hints had
been dropped, that if he did go there he might expect to be
handled somewhat roughly. The clergyman however did
go. He proposed to stop at the house of an acquaintance
who was quite an excitable character. Before entering the
house, he heard that one of the agitators on the other side of
the question had been there in the morning. He of course
then expected a scene of a good deal of excitement, and he
was by no means disappointed. Hardly had he entered
when his friend rushed up to him, and exclaimed: "Well,
sir, it is all over now!" "What is over." "There is going
to be a draft." "Well, what of that?" "We will not go!"
"But you will be made to go." "What, make fifty thousand men go?" "Ah remember my friend, it is not every

one thinks in this way. It is only a little corner here of Pennsylvania." "But," exclaimed the other with great vehemence, "I will not fight for the nigger!" "Not fight for the nigger," said my friend. "Well, now, listen to me. Suppose I were a general of the Secessionists, and had fifty thousand troops under my command, and I were standing here, and you were a general of the Union troops, and you had fifty thousand men under your command, and you were standing over there. And now suppose that you had learnt that here back of my right wing I had stored a vast deal of ammunition, and that you knew a way how to get round there and take it away from me, you also knowing that if you did take it, I would have no powder to fire at you, would you take it?" "Certainly!" "And then suppose that you had learnt that back of my left wing I had stored a considerable amount of provisions, and that you had an opportunity of getting hold of it, you knowing that if you succeeded in taking it, I would have to do with half rations and might be very much disposed to give up the fight; would you go and take it?" "Surely I would!" "And then again suppose, that far in the rear of me, there were five thousand negroes constantly at work in order to supply me with the provisions I needed, and that you knew a way how to catch them, and that you knew that if you did catch them, I was sure to give up, for I would have nothing whatever to eat. Would you go and catch them?" "Surely I would." "Well, that is all the Government proposes to do." "Is that all?" "Yes." "Well I am for that!" So it is, my reader, those who declare that the Government is no longer fighting for the Union and the Constitution are far from the truth. We have to accustom ourselves to the thought, that as matters now stand in the South, traitors have no right under the Constitution, and that the safety and the perpetuity of the Union, demand that they should be deprived of every means by which they are aided in their treasonable course. He who opposes the Government in this respect, is aiding and abetting treason, and to arrest such and punish them is the duty which the Government owes to the safety of its loyal citizens and to itself.

And this brings me to another branch of my subject. I have been often asked, what is likely to be the final result of all this loss of treasure and of blood. A similar question, I understand, one of my friends addressed the other day to a prominent individual in Washington. The person thus addressed was silent for a time, and then said with deep earnestness: "Our prophets are dead and I cannot tell." By the prophets he meant those great statesmen: Jefferson, Monroe, John Quincy Adams, Andrew Jackson, Clay, Webster and others, who in times gone by have been our political teachers, and who have pointed out to us the course we must take in order to enjoy peace and prosperity. But however interesting and touching this answer may appear, he could have given a better one. He could have said: "Our prophets are dead, and yet they speak." They speak by their example, and by the writings which they have bequeathed to us. Jefferson when he had been elected President said in his inaugural address: "We have called those who are our brothers, and who hold the same principles with ourselves by different names," referring thus mildly to the spirit of party which had been manifested previous to the election. Monroe when he had been President for four years, had so acted in the spirit of the words of Jefferson, that when his re-election was to take place, there was none to oppose him; the whole people formed a great American Union party. When Jackson, the democrat, had to contend against the doctrine of separation as promulgated by South Carolina, there stood by his side, Daniel Webster, the whig, and proved, particularly in his celebrated speech against Colonel Hayne of South Carolina, that the Constitution does not confer the right upon a single State, to cut loose from the Union at its pleasure. And when, on another occasion, again the safety of the Union was imperilled, it was Henry Clay, the whig, who expressed his gratitude to certain democratic members, because in the hour of danger they had set aside all considerations of party, and had aided him in preserving the Union. Nor would I forget John Quincy Adams, who, when he entered upon his presidential career, declared that no man who bore a good character and was fit for the office he held, should be deprived of it from considerations of party, and who acted in accordance with this declaration. Though dead, they speak. They tell us that now as in the time of Jefferson there are those, who, though they are called by different names, are yet our brethren, who are holding the same principles with us: they admonish us, that when the existence of the Union is at stake, we for a time at least ought to keep up our party lines less strictly, taking for our platform the *Union* as our forefathers have done; they speak to those in power and tell them that in the choice of the men they employ, they ought to be guided by merit and not by party considerations, and they speak to those who hold responsible positions under the Government, and remind them that they are bound to carry out the policy of the Government, independent of the fact that their associations of party would lead them in a different direction. It is this ground which the Union men of East Tennessee desire to occupy. When one of our wealthy slaveholders, after months of imprisonment, had returned, he was one day near his house, sitting upon a fence. Some Confederate soldiers were passing by, and one of them called to him to shout for Jefferson Davis. My friend refused to do so. "Are you for Lincoln?" asked the other. "I am for the Union," answered my friend, "and if Lincoln is for the Union, then am I for Lincoln." The soldiers threatened to kill him, but at that time did not do it. The Union is with the Union men of East Tennessee the paramount question. Every other is secondary. They are willing to lose sight of all party distinctions for a time, if the safety of the Union should require it. In this connection, however, I must once more allude to the subject of slavery. As I have already had an opportunity of showing, they are willing to put up with slavery, if that should be most conducive to the welfare of the Union, and they are willing to do without it, if the good of the Union should require it. It was sentiments like these which I expressed the other day in a large Democratic meeting. "Ah," said one of my hearers, "then that is just as Mr. Lincoln says: 'The Union with slavery, if that be best, the Union partly with and partly without slavery if that be best, the Union without slavery, if that be best; the Union any way.'" And they all approved of the doctrine. I hope the time will come when sentiments like these, which were uttered by loyal men in Montgomery county in this State, will be generally entertained, and when we all shall feel the importance of that spirit of forbearance, which in past times has guided us safely through so many dangers.

Among the many means which are used to mislead and deceive men, few have been found more efficient than the declaration, which we hear so often repeated, that we want "the Constitution as it is, and the Union as it was." When these words are pronounced by certain individuals they are exceedingly significant. They mean nothing less than that this administration is an abolition administration, that it is the cause of the war, that from the beginning it has carried on the war to subjugate the South and to set the negroes free, that it is a tyrannical administration subverting the Constitution, and that there is no hope for this country unless this administration can be overturned, the war be stopped and the rights of the South be acknowledged. By it they mean to say that they look with approval upon every measure of the Southern leaders, while they have nothing but abuse for the administration and those who sustain it, that they deeply sympathize with Jefferson Davis and his followers, while the men who have been driven from their homes, they regard as traitors to the sacred cause of the South, upon whom they mean to heap public and private insults whenever an opportunity shall offer. Such is the meaning of the words: "The Constitution as it is and the Union as it was," when these words come from certain lips. It is the very essence of treason, busily engaged in stirring up civil war in the North, openly or secretly. When uttered by others it is done more thoughtlessly, and the principal idea connected with them seems the conviction, that we ought to make peace and go on as we did in former times. It would be well, however, if men who make use of these words would fairly determine what they ought to mean. I also say: Give me the Union as it was. "Give it to me, to use the language of a distinguished East Tennessean,* as it was, when Washington to suppress rebellion, sent into Western Pennsylvania fifteen thousand men under the command of his neighbor and friend General Lee. . . . . When Webster and Clay rallied to the support of Andrew Jackson, and sent treason whipped and abashed to its lair. When Millard Fillmore, called to account for the disposition of his fleets in the harbor of Charleston, replied, that he was not responsible for his official conduct to the Governor of South Carolina." Such "as it was" is the Union I desire. Do not speak to me of a Union, such as it was, when James Buchanan connived at the treason which the members of his Cabinet were plotting, or when John C. Breckinridge poured forth treason in the Senate of the United States. If it even were possible to restore such a Union, it would be utterly wanting in the elements necessary for its perpetuity. One of the leaders of Secession in East Tennessee, a young man full of self-conceit and a captain in the rebel army, visited the house of one of our aged Union men, a descendant of one of the revolutionary heroes. "Ah," said the military fop, strutting up and down the room, "you old men may indeed talk of Washington and of his time as you do, but we who are younger have been brought up under different influences, and we follow different teachers." It is even so, and it would be in vain to think of forming a Union with men, who utterly repudiate what to the American patriot are sentiments the most sacred and the most true. The South has to be taught that the falsehoods on which they attempt to erect their slavery empire are not strong enough to serve their purpose, and whenever they have been taught it, we may have a Union, as it was in the days of this country's glory, a Union, better fitted to bless the world than it ever has been before, because chastened and purified.

And there is still another representation made by designing men, in order to mislead those who are little acquainted with the condition of affairs in the South. It is said that if in consequence of the war the negroes are set free they will

* Speech of the Hon. Horace Maynard of Tennessee, delivered in the House of Representatives, January 31, 1863.

come to the North and will bring down the free labor of the North to a ruinous extent. I have lived but six years in the South, and I have seen slavery but in Tennessee, in Georgia and in portions of South Carolina, Virginia and Alabama. As far as my knowledge extends I am fully persuaded that statements such as the one referred to are utterly void of foundation. Let me say to my readers emphatically, that the impressions which many have here in the North concerning the slaves of the South are extremely erroneous. The negroes are attached to the South by many bonds which are not easily broken. The South they regard as their home, they greatly prefer its climate; there many of them have families to whom they are attached, and church relations which they highly value; there they have an opportunity of making a good living, with but little labor, and though many desire to be free and daily pray for the success of the Northern arms, yet there is not one of them, I believe, who would think of coming North after he has obtained his freedom, and is placed in circumstances which will permit him quietly to enjoy it. "I care little," said a wealthy slave-holder to me, shortly before I left East Tennessee, "whether my slaves are set free or not. If they were set free they would not leave me. I would pay them what is right, and they would continue to work my plantation."

Before concluding I may be permitted to make another brief reference to myself. I need not say that Germany is dear to me; in Germany rest the bones of my fathers; there have I lived the beautiful days of my childhood and early youth. In Germany there are now living those who are bound to me not only by the ties of blood, but by ties which reach far beyond the grave. Yet while Germany is dear to me, I have also learnt to love this country during the thirty-five years I have lived here. I love it because it has invited millions like myself to its hospitable shores: I love it because it has extended its protection not only in distant lands or on distant seas, but also in every humble valley and on every retired hillside. There the industrious farmer could quietly attend to his daily avocation, and in the evening return to the circle of his family, as I have done for years,

and there under his own vine and fig-tree he could look
forward to the time when he would peacefully close his life.
When it seemed to be placed beyond a doubt that the Union
had ceased to exist, the friends of the South came to me once
more, and told me that I could have now no objection to
unite with them. I replied, that when I came to this country,
I swore allegiance to *the Union*, that in case the Union had
indeed ceased to exist, I did not own allegiance either to the
South or to the North, that I would return to my native
land and there perhaps after many years, when far advanced
in life, I would take my children's children upon my knees,
and with streaming eyes I would tell them of a noble land,
a powerful Union, of which at one time I was a citizen.
Since I have come North and have once more met with old
friends, who with the fire of youth are ready to battle for the
Union, which has protected them for so many years, and
since I have been brought in contact with so many youthful
spirits who go to the field of battle with the same spirit
which filled the heroes of the past, I am strongly impressed
with the fact that this Union is by no means so near its
dissolution as some of my Southern friends seemed to think
it was, and with John Adams I am ready to say, "Sink or
swim, live or die, survive or perish, the fortunes of this
country shall be my fortunes!" I stood the other day on
the spot where Melchoir Mühlenburg, the founder of the
Lutheran church in the United States, had labored for many
years. There at the time of the revolution and on a certain
Sabbath he had stood in his pulpit and had preached Christ
and Him crucified; he descends from the pulpit, he puts off
his gown, and he stands there before his astonished congregation in full military costume. There is a time for
preaching, he says, and there is a time for fighting, and my
time for fighting has come." Many clergymen are now
following his example. I know not what may be in store
for me, but I am certain that I am in the path of duty in
addressing these words of solemn warning to such as may
choose to read them. In what I have written I have briefly
traced the misrepresentations by which the leaders of the
South have succeeded in deceiving the great mass of the

people and the misery which has been the result of it. If the same spirit of deception should be successful here as it has been in the South, then the picture I have drawn of East Tennessee will be reflected in the valleys and on the hill-sides of Pennsylvania, we shall have here indeed the consti-tution as it is, but as it is in the South with its armed mobs, its spirit of indiscriminate plunder and its deeds of violence, and we shall no longer worry about the danger of having the slaves coming North, for we shall be *all* slaves, ruled with an iron rod by our Southern masters, and by those few Northern sympathizers and demagogues whom anarchy will make masters instead of slaves.

And now, in conclusion, I shall be permitted to make another brief reference to one of our "prophets." It is Daniel Webster, who in closing the speech, in which he proves that the constitution is not a compact between sov-ereign States, dwells in a strain of touching sadness on the possible future of the United States if the friends of nullifi-cation should be able to give practical effect to their opinions. "They would prove themselves in his judgment, the most skilful architects of ruin, the most effectual extinguishers of high raised expectations, the greatest blasters of human hopes that any age has produced. They would stand forth to proclaim in tones which would pierce the ears of half the human race, that the last experiment of representative gov-ernment had failed . . . . Millions of eyes, of those who now feed their inherent love of liberty on the success of the American example, would turn away on beholding our dismemberment, and find no place on earth whereon to rest their gratified sight. Amidst the incantations and orgies of nullification, . secession, disunion and revolution would be celebrated the funeral rites of constitutional and republican liberty!" I am thankful that it is not my task to trace in detail how much of the ruin which Daniel Webster thus anticipated has actually come to pass. Mine is a more cheerful task. However heart-rending the struggle may be through which we are passing, it is not a hopeless struggle to him who looks higher than the earth for a solution of it. If we see many things passing away which long familiarity has endeared to us, it is that they may be supplanted by higher and better ones. When the city of Geneva, threatened by the Duke of Savoy, the Pope and the Emperor, was reduced to the greatest weakness, its inhabitants still remained undismayed. "Geneva," they said, "is in danger of being destroyed, but God watches over us; better have war and liberty than peace and servitude; we do not put our trust in princes, and to God alone be the honor and glory!" How important the lesson which Geneva then was learning, and how well for us if we prove equally teachable, if we also learn to put our trust more fully in God than we have been disposed to do, fearful as the trials may be through which we may have to pass, we shall not be left without help. But in this respect also our prophets are our teachers. The sentiments with which Daniel Webster closed the speech, I have referred to, and which are conceived in this spirit we are fearlessly to put into action. "With my whole heart I pray for the continuance of the domestic peace and quiet of the country. I desire, most ardently, the restoration of affection and harmony to all its parts. I desire that every citizen of the whole country may look to this government with no other sentiments than those of grateful respect and attachment, but I cannot yield even to kind feelings the cause of the constitution, the true glory of the country, and the great trust which we hold in our hands for succeeding ages. If the constitution cannot be maintained without meeting these scenes of commotion and contest however unwelcome, they must come. We cannot, we must not, we dare not omit to do that which in our judgment, the safety of the Union requires . . . . I am ready to perform my own appropriate part, whenever and wherever the occasion may call on me, and to take my chance among those upon whom blows may fall first and fall thickest. I shall exert every faculty I possess in aiding to prevent the constitution from being nullified, destroyed or impaired: and even should I see it fall, I will still with a voice feeble, perhaps, but earnest as ever issued from human lips, and with fidelity and zeal which nothing shall extinguish, call on the PEOPLE to come to its rescue."

SKETCHES OF EAST TENNESSEE LIFE.

SKETCHES OF EAST TENNESSEE LIFE.

"East Tennessee ! Secluded land,
Of gentle hills and mountains grand,
Where healthful breezes ever blow,
And coolest springs and rivers flow ;
Where yellow wheat and waving corn
Are liberal poured from plenty's horn,—
Land of the valley and the glen,
Of lovely maids and stalwart men ;
Thy gorgeous sunsets well may vie,
In splendor with Italian sky.

*　　*　　*　　*　　*　　*

Enchanting land ! where nature showers
Her fairest fruits and gaudiest flowers ;
Where stately forests wide expand,
Inviting the industrious hand,
And all the searching eye can view
Is beautiful and useful too ;—
Who knows thee well, is sure to love,
Where'er his wandering footsteps rove,
And backward ever turns to thee,
With fond regretful memory ;
Feeling his heart impatient burn
Among thy mountains to return !"

"*East Tennessee.* By an East Tennessean."

WHEN, on a certain occasion, the opinion of a distinguished theologian was quoted, the reply given was, that that had been his opinion the year before, implying thereby that the theologian in question was somewhat noted for frequently changing his opinions. Many have said and felt that within the last three or four years they have been very much in the condition of the theologian referred to, having changed not only their opinions, but some of their most cherished convictions. I am well aware that in this respect I do not form an exception to the general rule, and I can only express the hope that my readers will find that if I have changed, I have not changed without a cause.

As these are the days of romantic adventure and of hair-breadth deliverances, I shall be very brief with regard to

(27)

the dangers which I encountered in making my escape from East Tennessee.

On Saturday, the 25th of April, 1862, I had reason to expect that several armed men were in search of me. About eleven o'clock, A. M., I left my house without changing my dress, in order to give the impression to those I met that I was not embarking on a long journey. I reached the house of a Union man and there staid over night. When on the next morning I came to the Clinch river, I found that river had been stripped by the rebels of all the canoes and ferry boats. I was in imminent danger of being discovered and arrested, when a slave informed me that another slave had concealed a boat in order to visit his wife who lived on the other side of the river. An arrangement was made that the slave should come to a certain spot on Monday morning before daylight, so that I might reach a place of safety before the rebel cavalry entered upon their daily work of scouring the country.

Long before day I was at the appointed spot. I waited and waited, and had given up almost all hope, when I heard the noise of the approaching boat, and soon afterwards saw it coming towards me. Little can I describe the revulsion of feeling which I at that moment experienced. The sun had risen, and for more than an hour the birds on the trees around me had welcomed him; the river had been peacefully flowing at my feet; the cattle had gone forth to graze on the meadows and the hills before me; a scene of rare beauty had courted my attention, but I had had ear and eye only for the boat which was to take me to a place of safety.

I was then about thirteen miles from my home, ten miles more I had been told would bring me to the house of B. R.,* and with him I would be safe. I walked as fast as I well could; at last I could walk no further. A few hundred yards from the house I wished to reach I had sat down to rest, when a horseman rode up to me. I told him that I was on my way to B. R. "I am B. R.," replied he. "Then with you I am safe." "Not with me; my son-in-law is a Con-

---

* These are not the initials of the name of the man here referred to.

federate soldier, you would be arrested the moment you entered my house." He then showed me a path by which I might avoid being seen from his house, and which would take me to a place of safety. The path referred to led up to the top of a steep mountain. As I slowly ascended it I again and again went to the margin of the woods in order to find out whether I might still be discovered from the house I was endeavoring to avoid. It seemed to me as if I could not get out of its reach, and my excited imagination seemed to discover some one on the watch for me at each of its windows. At last, however, I arrived at the top of the mountain, the house was still in sight, but so far below me that no eye from thence could reach my place of safety. Then I fell on my knees and thanked God.

On Monday night I enjoyed the hospitality of a Union family, and on Tuesday I left Anderson county and crossed into Scott county. In the year 1860, I had travelled through this county as agent of the Bible Society, and had become intimately acquainted with its inhabitants, as well as with several of its mountain passes. Little had I anticipated that my escape from imprisonment or death would be facilitated by the friends to whom I then ministered and by the intimate knowledge of the country which I then acquired. On Wednesday morning I stood once more on the mountain which overlooks Powell's Valley and at the foot of which lies the town of Jacksboro, the county seat of Campbell's county. Down that valley I had often gone on the way to my home. This time, however, my course lay in a different direction. I descended the north side of the mountain and passing down Elk creek valley reached on Thursday morning the East Tennessee troops at Camp Spears on the line of Campbell county, Tenn., and Whitley county, Ky. In the following week, when the men who had been in pursuit of me called for the third time at my house in quest of me, my wife had received information of my safe arrival at the Federal army, and was cheered by the thought that I was beyond the reach of capture. In that week also, I received news from home. So active, was at that time, the secret intercourse between our army and the Union men of East Tennessee.

Two years and a half had passed when I was permitted to visit once more the home I had been compelled to leave so suddenly. Great, indeed, was the change which in the meantime had taken place. On the 22d of October of this year it was my privilege to stand in the Court House in the city of Knoxville in the same spot where three years before I had seen the rebel Judge Humphreys, and arraigned before him a number of Union men. I there had heard the State's attorney make the charge and the Judge pronounce the sentence, while the rebel flag which was within that hall told of the mockery of justice which was going on there. Where now was the Judge? Where the State's attorney? Where the crowd of rebels that filled that hall, and where the band of soldiers that surrounded that rebel flag? They were gone, and Union men who at that time were ever on the lookout for a hiding place from the bitter hatred of these men could now freely assemble. Equally great was the change which had taken place outside of that hall. Where was the glorious "chivalry" which so proudly walked these streets, taking special pleasure in insulting Union men after they robbed them of their arms? Where the distinguished orators who were ever ready in set speech to laud the " noble defenders" for going where they did not mean to go? Where the staunch friends of the rebel cause, who freely gave their money for it, or, if they loved their money too well, their best wishes? And where those apostles of a new dispensation which was to establish a mighty empire on the glorious and everlasting foundation of the divine institution of slavery? They were gone, and in their places I beheld the familiar faces of the Union men and women of East Tennessee, protected by East Tennessee and Northern troops, over whom were floating the Stars and Stripes. A portion of the garrison consisted of colored troops, and many of those whom I had known as slaves, from various reasons, were slaves no more, and were handsomely supporting their families by their industry.

Yet while a favorable change had taken place in the condition of the Union men of East Tennessee, there was room left for improvement. I encountered in the streets of Knoxville those who had been leaders in the cause of the rebellion. Some of them, though they had taken the oath of amnesty, were still breathing the old spirit of hostility to the Union. I told one of them that he had committed a great wrong against his country. He replied that that remained yet to be seen. Another, who knew not my political position, declared that he was as great a rebel as ever, that he had a right to be a rebel, and that he was ready to do over again all that he had done. Shortly before my arrival in Knoxville, some of these men had been guilty of such acts of violence, that the Union men had been compelled to take the law into their own hands. One of the results of this course is a change of residence on the part of many. Of this I received a some- what striking proof in meeting incidentally with one of my former neighbors. In the dark days of December in 1861, this neighbor had come to my house, and in the course of a long conversation he had told me that I now clearly saw that the men of the North were a set of cowards; they would not fight, and all the South had to do was to draw a line along the Ohio river, to erect fortifications opposite Cincinnati, and whenever the North stole a negro to fire right into the city. On revisiting East Tennessee I happened to call at his house. I found him and his whole family on the point of moving to the North. He could not stay in East Tennessee, he said, two shots had been fired into his house. I asked him what had become of the line he intended to draw along the Ohio river. He thought that was all over. I gave him a line to a friend of mine at the North, and felt, while doing it, that the country would gain more, if some greater transgressor than he were removed from within its borders.

But I turn to brighter aspects of the picture I am drawing. Whenever we glance at the mineral wealth of the United States we are generally disposed to give free scope to our thoughts; starting at the Rocky mountains we rest not till they have arrived at the Sierra Nevada. I appreciate the fact that in the Western states and territories, the government of the United States is still the sole proprietor of this exhaustless wealth. Yet I am not disposed to undervalue on that account the mineral wealth of Tennessee and of the states which border on it. Let the war be ended and there will come with free labor the spirit of enterprise and the liberal use of capital. Let this mountain region be joined to Cincinnati by a railroad passing through the Cumberland Gap, and to Philadelphia by one passing through Western Virginia, and as by the magic wand of some mighty wizard, the iron, the coal, the nitre, the zink, the lead, the copper, the saltpetre, the salt, and the marble of this region will be brought to light. With the cotton region in their immediate vicinity, the streams which now flow down these mountains in idle beauty, will be made to turn the wheels of numberless manufactures, while the generous fruit of the vine will cover those mountain sides. Cities, towns and villages will be linked to each other by the common interest of commercial enterprise, and as schools and churches, and the faithful labors of an enlightened ministry are multiplied, these mighty mountain fastnesses, which God Himself has formed, will be manned by a population capable of doing their part in guarding the temporal, moral, and spiritual interests of the nation. The rebels have made light of many losses, but they have never made light of the loss of East Tennessee. According to the rebel press, it was the hardest blow that had been struck them since the beginning of the war, for the possession of East Tennessee admitted the enemy to the very vitals of the Confederacy "What," they asked, "is to become of the Southern armies, if they are deprived of the nitre, the coal, the iron, the saltpetre, the lead, and the salt of East Tennessee? How are they to be fed without her cattle and her hogs?" And louder than any testimony of the rebel press on this point, speak Chickamauga, Missionary Ridge, Lookout Mountain, and the desperate assaults of Longstreet on Knoxville.

In noticing the steps which have been taken to prepare this better state of things, I would not willingly pass by the generous spirit with which the North has come to the help of East Tennessee. Again and again I learned from the lips of those who are best acquainted with the history of these benevolent movements, that but for this timely help many would have died from want of food. The Rev. T. W. Humes, of the Episcopal Church, who, at the time I left East Tennessee in 1861, was not excepted from the persecution which more or less visited every faithful Union man, I found devoted to this work. By his personal influence he had kept in combined and benevolent action elements, which, in many respects, seemed to harmonize but little. In now recalling, on the one hand, the scenes of suffering which I witnessed in the two "homes" for refugees in the city of Knoxville, and, on the other, the abundance of means enjoyed by some of those who had been most active in producing these sufferings, the question readily presents itself whether the wealth which these men have obtained in rebelling against their country might not be made to contribute to the relief of those who have lost their all.

The interest felt by those who have suffered oppression and persecution has not been confined to the narrow bounds of East Tennessee. Other portions of our country have justly come in for their share of attention. I hardly know a better way to impress us with a sense of the blessings we enjoy than by contrasting them with the scene of suffering and want which the Union Commission of the city of New York has drawn. Yet while all deserve attention, I still trust that the fact will not be left out of sight that the late incursion of the rebels and the inclemency of the season, must greatly add to the suffering of East Tennessee.

Having made these statements concerning the present condition and the probable future of East Tennessee, and of the mountain region, of which it forms a part, I cannot but dwell briefly on some of the topics which they call to mind. I have referred to some of them on a former occasion, but the events which have since taken place have in a measure modified the views I have expressed.

When, in the spring of 1861, the rebellion broke out, and found me in the South, and when for months afterwards our very existence as a nation seemed in danger, I felt disposed to turn away from the present, which had for me nothing but sorrow, in order to dwell on the happier days of the past.

For months I occupied myself almost exclusively with the works of those who had founded or defended the institutions of this country. I came here when John Quincy Adams occupied the Presidential Chair; I had admired the course taken by Andrew Jackson when he encountered the spirit of Secession; step by step at my humble distance, I had followed Henry Clay and Daniel Webster in their struggles for the Union. To them my heart now turned, and to them I looked for light. But when I had reached the North, and there beheld the energy and hopefulness of the great mass of the people, and the readiness with which they brought every sacrifice; when in my daily intercourse with the sick, the wounded and the dying soldiers, I received the most elevating and touching proofs of the patriotism by which they were animated, I learned to feel, that if other ages had their peculiar tasks allotted to them, so must ours have, and I was led to inquire, whether perchance I had not been led into serious errors. For more than twenty years of my life I had sided with those friends of the Union, who had granted to the slaveholders whatever they demanded in order to secure to them the possession of their slaves, yet in spite of all this, these slaveholders had attempted to break to pieces the Union for which they had professed so ardent a love. Had I been mistaken in my course? Was there something in the very character of slavery which would necessarily produce such results? I had laughed at the idea of an irrepressible conflict between slavery and freedom; was there, after all, some truth in it. I will not detain the reader with the particulars of the examination in which I engaged in order to obtain a satisfactory answer to these inquiries. Suffice it to state some of its results.

To some it may seem strange that it was only after some reading, and after having passed through a certain moral and intellectual struggle, that I arrived at the conclusion that the error into which I had fallen, and which lay at the foundation of much that had been wrong in my political course, consisted in this: that I had shut my eyes against the truth, that the Creator has breathed into every human soul the right of life and of liberty; that I had failed to see that

God could never have intended that man whom he had created in his own image, should be treated as a piece of property. In the light of this truth I was no longer without the means of judging why those who had established this Government had suffered the seeds of discord to mingle with it. The practice of enslaving men had produced the effect which every transgression of the divine law produces; it had hardened the hearts and darkened the minds of those who had been engaged in or had countenanced this traffic. To this must be ascribed the fact, that at the time when the Constitution was framed, there were Southern States to be found who did not hesitate to demand that security should be given them, so that they might continue the African slave trade undisturbedly, and that the convention gave them that security for twenty years more. And to this must also be ascribed that other fact that with the question of representation the claim of certain Southern States had come up, that their slaves, though they regarded them as property should be represented in Congress, and that that claim also had been granted as far as three-fifths of the slave population were concerned.

It does not belong to me on the present occasion to present in detail the consequences which followed from these worse than unwise measures. Mine is not the sad task of tracing the gradual progress of the spirit of selfishness in many of its worst forms, which the existence of slavery served to excite and to foster. It is only a brief reference to this subject which comes within my scope.

I have, on a former occasion, dwelt on the fact that in consequence of the competition of slave labor the emigrants from abroad preferred settling in the North, that in the same measure as Slave States were added to the Union, they added also to the weakness of the South, and that finding the struggle utterly unequal, the South had resolved to destroy the Union by seceding from it. I have spoken of the spirit which animated the thousands who rushed to the field of battle after Fort Sumter had fallen, and of the issuing of the proclamation of emancipation as a military measure, in order to deprive the rebellion of its principal means of support.

These topics have been widely discussed, and on that account are well known to most of my readers. It is not so easy to trace the less apparent influences in consequence of which a large portion of the people of the United States hold now a position with regard to slavery which is very different from the ground which they occupied at the beginning of the rebellion. It is on account of the change which has thus generally taken place, that I have felt less hesitation to prove by the remarks which I have made, that I am not an exception to the general rule. The moral and intellectual torpor in which the great mass of the people of the United States have been with regard to the subject of slavery, and the suddenness with which they have been roused, surpasses in strangeness the marvellous tale of the sleeper of Manhattan, and it is not wonderful that some amongst those who have been thus suddenly aroused should hardly know what they say or do, and should forget that there are other sins besides the sin of slavery of which we, as a nation, have to repent in order to enjoy the favor of God.

From the course which the South has pursued it is evident that if we seek for the men to whom the abolition of slavery must be ascribed, we must not go to Maine, Massachusetts or Ohio, but to the home of Jefferson Davis, and to those who with him have stirred up this rebellion. As for myself, my teachers have been the effects which slavery has produced on those who own slaves, and on the masses of the people who do not own them, but who are injured by being brought in close and constant contact with the institution. On me, also, the shot fired at Fort Sumter has produced a lasting impression, and I can now understand why it was that on first visiting the South, it was not without a choking sensation that I could ask a colored man whose property he was, or why I was strenuously in favor of the fugitive slave law, and yet equally determined not to interfere with any slave who might endeavor to get away. I had left unheeded the irrepressible conflict in my own heart.

In summing up these somewhat desultory observations I shall once more refer to one whom I always honored, but whom the convulsions of our time have taught me to appre-

ciate far more highly than I had done till that time. I came
to this country in 1828. Five or six years before that time,
John Quincy Adams had summed up the views he entertained on the subject of slavery, by stating that it would not
be difficult to prove, that all that had been done to the honor
of this country had been done in spite of slavery, and all
that had been dishonorable to it had been done by the means
of slavery. In view of the light which the rebellion sheds
on the history of this country, I am ready to adopt the words
of John Quincy Adams, with regard to the years which have
gone by since he wrote them, and to say that it is high time
to abolish an institution which has been the means of causing
so much evil and of inflicting so much injury.

The influence which the introduction of free labor will
have in the South is likely, among many others, to produce
two effects. I have already attended to the fact that it will
do away with that undue deference with which for many
years past the "chivalry" of the South have been treated·
It will also set us right with regard to many questions concerning the colored people, which now seem difficult of solution. There may be much hesitation in various quarters, but
public opinion will decide at last that men are not to be
judged by the color of their skin, but by their hearts and
their conduct. Men may be alarmed at the thought, that if
this maxim were to prevail, it must lead to the strangest
results. "What," they may ask, "will become of society
when the colored people are suffered to mingle freely with
the whites, when the right of citizenship is extended to a
race, which learned divines as well as physicians equally
learned, have declared to be an inferior one? And what
especially will become of those Southern States, where the
colored people are in the majority. These, and many similar
questions will be brought more and more to the test of history
and I fear not the result. The vast immigration which free
labor will invite to the South, and the spirit with which it is
likely to be animated, will dispose of them all. A partial
solution of this difficulty, however, we are receiving from
day to day, The better sense and the better feeling of the
people will not rest till the merits of this case are placed in

their proper light. When the rebellion first broke out in the South we feared that the blacks would rise and butcher the whites. How different from this has been the spirit of humanity by which they have been animated! When ·the question of employing them in the army first came up, what an amount of ridicule was showered upon them, yet how plainly has their conduct shown how undeserving they were of it! Can I forget that when white men sought my ruin, it was a colored man who saved me from imprisonment or death? And what a volume the record of those would make whom the colored people have saved in a similar manner. There is, on this subject, a certain clinging to prejudice, expressed but too often in a way by no means elevated, which may be met among a portion of our foreign population. It is shared by not a few Americans who move in a sphere which makes their willingness to be swayed by prejudice far less excusable. But the more generous feeling of the great mass of the people will do away with this spirit, or at least make it powerless of evil.

The spirit manifested by the great mass of the people in the midst of the gigantic struggle for its very life in which they are engaged is also a pledge of the better future which I anticipate. At the beginning of this struggle, when the rebellion seemed to be successful, I, like others, had been led to doubt the power of the people for self-government. My experience in the progress of it fills me with new hope. As for the Presidential election it is certain that the right of free discussion has not been improperly infringed, and the question at issue has been settled by the enlightened judgment and the determined will of a vast majority of the people. The sight of a nation involved in a fearful civil war, and peacefully at the ballot-box choosing the man who is to lead them to final victory and peace, may well fill us with hope. While this canvass was going on, I again and again received messages from my friends at the front, telling me that we need not fear concerning them; that they would do their share by the sword to preserve the integrity of the country, but that they appealed to their friends at home not to be unmindful of their duty.

They at the front might win victory after victory in *this* war, but they could do no more, while the loyal men at home had it in their power to crush the seed, which if suffered to take root and to grow up would flood the country in blood for many years to come. With humble gratitude to God we now send back to them the cheerful tidings that we have fought the battle and that the battle has been won.

There is a tombstone erected in Spain on the grave of Columbus which says that Columbus has given a continent to the crown of Spain. It is Daniel Webster who, with regard to this inscription has said that Columbus has done more: he has given that continent to the world! Millions of emigrants have said the same and have felt it more deeply. Many a soldier from distant lands has been found ready to sacrifice health and life to secure to the world that precious gift. The aim of the slave power has been to restrict this gift of Columbus and "to exclude from a vast unoccupied region emigrants from Europe and free laborers from our own States and to convert it into a dreary region inhabited by masters and slaves." The question has often been asked, how, in view of this fact so many of the European emigrants can favor the continuation of slavery? It is a question which admits of an answer, but this is not the place to give it.

In conclusion, I shall draw from the storehouse of the past two scenes, which have reference to Andrew Johnson, an East Tennessean, now Vice President elect of the United States.

In the Spring of 1861, Governor Andrew Johnson, then a Senator of the United States, was addressing a large assembly of Union men in one of the streets of the city of Knoxville. While doing so, John D. Crozier, formerly a member of Congress and now a fugitive in the South, endeavored to induce a company of rebel cavalry who were then in town to fall upon the Union men. Several prominent citizens, though strongly in favor of the rebellion, succeeded in preventing the catastrophy. This is the first scene.

The second is this: On the 8th of June of the year 1864. I found myself in the midst of a vast crowd in one of the halls of the city of Baltimore. Abraham Lincoln had been unanimously nominated President of the United States, and the time had come to nominate the Vice President Soon after the voting had commenced shout after shout was heard, and with these shouts was mingling the name of Andrew Johnson. A few minutes later he was unanimously nominated Vice President of the United States. As I heard it and thought of the scenes of humiliation through which Andrew Johnson had passed, I remembered that "God resisteth the proud but giveth grace to the humble."

I know no thought better than this with which to conclude. In the changes which our time is bringing about, not only christians but men of the world are constrained to recognize the agency of a higher power, and to declare that this is indeed "the Lord's doing, and that it is marvellous in our eyes."

It is this humble reliance on the power of God, which is the only sure pledge of the safety and perpetuity of this Nation.

LIFE AND DEATH OF A CHRISTIAN SOLDIER

A SKETCH OF THE LIFE AND DEATH OF

CORPORAL CHARLES CRARY.

WE deem it not strange when here and there a monument is erected to some soldier who has cheerfully laid down his life for his country; and the distinction thus conferred on a few does not, in our estimation, take away one iota from the glory which belongs to those who fought as bravely, but who sleep in unknown graves. In like manner does a sketch of the life and the death of one and the other of our departed soldiers by no means lessen the gratitude which we feel for thousands of others, who have fought and died equally well, but of whose deeds or sufferings we know little or nothing.

The conduct of the late Corporal Charles Crary, during the four weeks which preceded his death, was of such a character that it made a very deep and solemn impression on the minds of the few who became acquainted with him at that time, and I even then felt a strong desire to give publicity to the closing scenes of his life, that the influence of his example might be extended beyond the circle of those who had been brought in personal contact with him. The daily calls of duty have prevented my sooner carrying out this intention. At last, however, I have been enabled to prepare this sketch. I present it to the public with the earnest prayer, that it may be accompanied by the Spirit of God, and that it may do good to the hearts of many.

The spirit of depression which had pervaded the community during the latter part of June, 1863, had been changed into a spirit of joy and gratitude. The account of the victory of Gettysburg had been succeeded by the tidings from Vicksburg, announcing that that stronghold had fallen. But with this joy was mingled a feeling of sadness. Our loss had been very great; and, as far as the battle of Gettysburg was concerned, we were soon to obtain visible evidence of some of its effects by the wounded who were to be placed within the walls of our hospitals. We had not to wait long. Arrival succeeded arrival; and on the 12th of July, every bed in the Turner's Lane Hospital was occupied.

As I passed from ward to ward, and engaged in conversation with every one who was able to converse, I found that I had before me representatives of almost every portion of the army by whom the "Three Days" battle had been fought. Here was one who had been engaged in the unequal conflict in which Reynolds fell. Here another who had fought under Howard, when that General, with Schurz's and Barlow's divisions, came to the relief of the First corps. A third had been engaged with Wadsworth when this general repulsed the enemy. Some had been with Slocum and Sickles, and had been wounded in the conflict which took place the second day; others had been with Geary, when he drove Ewell from the foothold which the latter had gained at Spangler's Spring; and still others had been wounded on the third day, when the fearful struggle was going on which terminated in the repulse of Longstreet, Hill and Pickett. The condition in which many of them were, was well calculated to call forth my deepest sympathies. Among them was a young man who had lost both his eyes, and who was endeavoring to soothe his pain by repeating passages of Scripture and hymns which he had learnt in his childhood; another had been wounded in the knee in a manner which did not admit of an operation. He was unceasingly engaged in earnest prayer; still another, feeling death to be near, was sending his last messages to one he loved. I had arrived nearly at the end of the last ward, when I approached a young man who, I was told, had been shot through the right lung. In my conversation with him, I alluded to the comfort to be derived from faith in the Lord Jesus Christ, when he joyfully testified that for years that faith had been his support. This was Corporal Charles Crary. In his case, as in

the case of so many others, the attack made upon Fort
Sumter had given rise to thoughts and emotions, which,
thousands of times, have since then been eloquently expressed
in poetry and in prose, but which on that account do not lose
in force or beauty when coming from the lips of a dying
soldier. The country, which to him had seemed more firmly
established than other, had been threatened with dissolution;
the flag, which to him had been the emblem of power at
home and abroad, had been dishonored; the Union, which
had been endeared to him from the days of his earliest childhood, had been rejected with scorn and contempt. The
calumnies and the insults with which the South had assailed
North, he had regarded with astonishment, but borne with
patience; but not for a moment could he endure the thought
that his country, with its free institutions, should be swept
away—that the flag, till then so highly honored, should
become the emblem of weakness and of shame, and that the
Union, which had been to him the cause of so many blessings, should be supplanted by a multitude of independent
States and cities, engaged in endless feuds against each other.
Charles Crary, to use his own words, had felt that his country
called him, and he could not but respond to the call. His
position in Detroit had had much to attach him to his home,
and to the circle of his friends—the relations with which he
stood to the church, of which he was a member—had been
of a peculiarly endearing character; his employment in a
printing office furnished him with sufficient support; yet he
had bade a cheerful farewell to all these in order to take his
share in the defence of his country. He enlisted in the 24th
Michigan Infantry on the 29th of July, 1861; and after
having taken part in the battles of Fredericksburg and
Chancellorville, he had been mortally wounded in the battle
of Gettysburg.

The letters which he had written previous to his removal
to the Turner's Lane Hospital, manifest a spirit of patriotic
devotion which is not the less beautiful, because it is united
with a strong love for his home, and an earnest devotion to
his God and Saviour. To one of his relations, who had
inquired why he had entered the army, he wrote: "I thought

I could see that the time had come for me to do my share to keep the glorious old ensign of the Republic up at his full height, and to help to suppress the rebellion against the Constitution's life."

In another letter he speaks of the good chaplain with whom the Twenty-fourth was favored, and of a custom adopted by the "boys" of his company. They would get together a short time before the retreat was beaten, and take turns in reading a chapter in the New Testament.

In the same strain he writes at another time: " in roving about the camp, when off duty, I have found one of the finest little spots, where I can retire when I wished to read, write, or rest, undisturbed: it is by the side of a little rippling brook which rises on the hillside, and is carpeted with nice green grass, and shaded by fine old trees, many of which are over-grown with grape-vines, giving it quite a romantic appearance."

On the 27th of November, a day of thanksgiving, his heart overflowed with gratitude over "hard tack and tough beef," and over the good effect which the toughening process of soldiering had on his health. In a letter written shortly after Christmas, and called forth partly by a Christmas-box, which had been sent to "dear brother Charley" from his home, he visits in imagination the circle of his loved ones; and, leaping over years of struggle, he sees the Twenty-fourth disembarking from the Cleveland boat, and marching up one of the streets of the city of Detroit, not so strong as when they left, but every man a soldier—the step steady and firm—waving over them the old flag tattered and torn, as well it might be. He hears the cheers of welcome, he thanks God that the war is over, and at the familiar sound of "Break ranks, march!" he knows well what line of march one of the number of that regiment is taking. At another time, in writing to his father, who had admonished him to keep up good courage and to take care of his health, he writes in a strain which shows that his gentle nature could be easily roused whenever placed face to face with disloyalty. "I do not think," he writes, "my courage will need much propping so long as there are rebels in arms; and although the cause of the Union looks a little cloudy now, on account of the rebels holding out so persistently at Vicksburg, I have full faith that it must fall, and with it the dearest hopes of the Confederates."

In a similar manner he speaks, in another letter, of the contempt with which the army regards those in the North who are guilty of disloyalty. "Soldiers," he writes, "who offer their lives in defence of their country will not forget traitors, who, in their absence, are using every effort to undo their work. . . You may well say, 'The army is a unit.'"

These quotations exhibit the spirit which pervades all the letters of Charles Crary. Cool on the day of battle, and patient when suffering from severe exposure, he was yet unwilling that his loved ones at home should be troubled on account of the dangers to which he was exposed. In consequence of it, there is constantly mingling in these letters that disregard of self which characterizes the brave soldier and that tenderness for others which belongs to the loving heart.

The letter which he wrote after he had received his death-wound, will be better appreciated by the reader after he has perused the following account of some of the occurrences which took place at that period. It has been prepared, at my request, by Mr. James F. Clegg, also of the 24th, who had been his constant companion from the time they both had enlisted together in the city of Detroit, and who had been wounded in the same battle:

"The Twenty-fourth Michigan is one of the regiments composing the old 'Iron Brigade' of General Meredith. It was in Wadsworth's First division of the First army corps, commanded at that time by General Reynolds. This brigade is one of the oldest in the Army of the Potomac, and has distinguished itself on many battle-fields. Having arrived near Gettysburg, the First corps moved from a point about five miles south of Gettysburg, on Wednesday morning, the 1st of July, the Iron Brigade at the head. Charley and I marched along the road till we came within a mile of Gettysburg, when we heard the first shot of the great battle, and saw the explosion of a shell directly over the house of Dr. Schmucker, to the right of the Seminary. We turned to the left, and double-quicked it up to Willoughby's Run, and across the Hagerstown road. We relieved the cavalry, who had been skirmishing previous to our arrival, and climbed the little hill east of the run. General Reynolds fell about this time, and Doubleday took command. We scarce reached the crest when we received a volley from a concealed foe; and with orders, the regiment fixed bayonets, loaded, fired, and charged, capturing a large number of rebels in the ravine. I noticed that Charley appeared more serious this morning than usual; his manner was more earnest; he performed his duty with his usual alacrity, but his countenance showed determination, rather than the *fire* visible on similar occasions. We took position in the woods on the bank of Willoughby's Run. We were not in the position given by many charts of that field, but were on the extreme left of the corps. One regiment only—the Nineteenth Indiana—being left of the Twenty-fourth.

The corps lay in the woods perhaps two or three hours, with some skirmishing between the pickets, when the rebel army emerged from the woods about three hundred yards in front. Three lines advanced upon our single line, and their right overlapped our left perhaps a quarter of a mile. The fighting commenced immediately, but the rebels continued to advance. The corps posted on our right falling back, we were flanked on the right: turning to the left, we saw the enemy almost in our rear. Being thus flanked on both sides, and in danger of being captured, we fell back slowly, firing constantly, forming and reforming lines, but only to be driven back again. For nearly a mile the brigade fought, and was always in rear of the retreating forces. Nine out of the 24th's color-bearers fell. The colonel seized them, planted them in the ground, and called to the regiment, now scattered over all the field, to rally round the colors. And they did—all who could hear him—and fought until the enemy were literally upon them, when the few left were also compelled to fall back. I saw Charley at this time; he fell but a minute afterwards. Our next meeting was in the Seminary Hospital, then held by the enemy. Two men carried him up toward the back steps, at about 5 o'clock

in the evening. Seeing him carried towards the hospital, I
ran out to assist him. The men left when they saw some
one who knew him. Charley expressed sorrow on seeing
me wounded, but pleasure at our being still together. A
stream of blood was slowly trickling down from his right
shoulder, and he was very weak. He rested that night in
the great hall of the Seminary, among the hundreds of
wounded who literally crammed it, and rendered night fearful by their groans and cries. Next morning he moved to
the recitation room, where he was much more comfortable,
for we occupied it alone. But it was dangerous at times;
for the enemy planted a battery at each corner of the hospital, and the return shots of our batteries frequently struck
the building. Some shots passed directly through the room
he was in. We were often compelled to leave the room and
seek shelter in the hall. Once the shells were exploding all
around the building, and I helped him to the hall; but we
had barely closed the door, when we heard a great explosion
in the room. I saw, when the firing ceased, a fragment of a
shell in the centre of the narrow bed he occupied. You
cannot imagine the relief we felt on Sunday, the 5th, when
daylight showed us that the rebel army had utterly disappeared. It was equalled only by the people in the town,
who for the first time had been forced to submit to this
terrible ordeal. It was some time before our wounds were
treated, for the enemy had taken all the surgical instruments
from our surgeons. Charley frequently asked to hear the
Holy Scriptures read; and from the old Bible in the teacher's
desk, I read to him such passages as he wished to hear. He
preferred the New Testament and Psalms. I remember one
which he often wished me to read (the 139th), and he always
would remain in meditation for some time after. He remained in the Seminary until the 9th, when the surgeon told
us that all who were able to leave must do so, and go to the
general hospitals. Charley did not wish to remain: he arose,
and with difficulty reached the depot. He expected to be
sent to Michigan, but was not displeased when he reached
Philadelphia, and was placed in the Turner's Lane Hospital, for
he feared the distance. He showed great interest in his

country's cause during the week of victories, and was always pleased to hear any one read of the progress of the war. I well remember the pride he showed when hearing of our corps' fighting on that day, and the sorrow when he heard of the great loss his own regiment had sustained: 'Only ninety of my five hundred comrades left!' "

While at the Seminary in Gettysburg he wrote the following letter, which, through the kindness of Mrs. Crary. is now before me. It is written with a pencil:

GETTYSBURG, PA., July 6th, 1863.

" DEAR MOTHER:—We have met the enemy and have driven him out of Pennsylvania. The fight was a hard one. I was struck in the shoulder July 1st, so as to deprive me of the use of my right arm for the present. I am doing well now, and think I shall be all right in a couple of months. Clegg is here also—wounded slightly in the right arm, between the elbow and the hand—no bone is broken. My wound is in rather a bad place, but the doctor says I will come out all right. I do not know what I would have done without Clegg's help. His wound is so slight that, except the use of his right arm, he is as good as new ware. As there were many worse than me, and so few doctors, and we in the rebels' hands part of the time (three days), I should have suffered but for him. But God is good. I am not very badly wounded, and in good health and spirits. I must close now, for it is hard work to write left-handed. . . . . There are but six men and no officers in our Company."

From these letters my readers are enabled to form some idea of the character of the subject of this sketch. What I have seen of him during my intercourse with him while in our hospital, filled me with a desire to know more of his early life. The light which the following extracts throw on this subject will, no doubt, prove generally interesting. They are taken from a letter which Mrs. Crary had the kindness to address to me in reply to one of mine. "The memory of that beloved boy," writes Mrs. Crary, "is indeed precious. He was but an infant when I first professed re-

ligion; and in the first warm gushing love of a new-born
soul, I felt a desire, not only to be myself the Lord's, but
that all I loved and cherished should also be His; and in my
heart I gave my first-born, my well-beloved little Charley,
to Him. The vow made secretly to my God alone, often
bore heavily on my soul, when I was careless or remiss in
nurturing and training him for the Lord. Oh! my dear
Christian brother, I cannot express to you the weight that
was on my heart, when I realized what a fearful reponsibility
I had taken upon myself. He was always a pleasant child:
but he grew to the age of fourteen without manifesting any
particular religious feeling. At that time he was away from
home at Franklin College, Indiana. There was a revival in
progress in the place we were then living (Lafayette, Indiana,)
and many were converted; and many who were in a cold
state, were brought to see their wickedness in departing
from the living God. I, too, was roused from lethargy, and
felt renewed anxiety for my child. At my earnest solicita-
tion his father consented to his return home before the close
of the term. Charley seemed to feel that there must be in
my mind some great anxiety for him. After he had attended
the meetings but a few days, he became very seriously impressed, and begged me to pray for him. At the prayer
meeting, held at our house the next morning, he felt that the
burthen of his sins was removed. I have never doubted
that he was then and there born unto the kingdom of God's
dear Son. His desire was to go immediatly forward and put
on Christ before the world; but his father a very careful
man, restrained him, fearing from his youth and the excited
state of his feelings, that he might think himself converted
when he was not. By his father's request he went back to
school, without uniting with any Church. About two years
after, unexpected reverses came upon us, and my husband was
obliged to close his business (mercantile), to meet his liabili-
ties. We found a new home, where we were obliged to live
on much less than my husband formerly paid his clerks. It
was the Lord's doings, and I thank him for *adversity*. This
trial which seemed so grievous, was for our good, and *proved*
to me my belief had been well founded, that Charley had the

grace of God in his heart. A few days after we had been settled here, he said to me, 'Well, mother, school is done with me. If father has to work for his bread, so have I.' 'But,' said I, 'my son, what can you do?' 'Whatever my hand findeth to do, I will do it with my might.' He went out, and when he returned, said, he had found work in a printing office. I do not know that he had ever visited one before, and expressed my fears of his success. He said, 'I shall try ;' and he did try, and remained in that same office until his enlistment in the defence of his country. When he left his situation, where he was receiving fifty dollars a month, he enlisted as a private. Nothing but filial affection had prevented his going when the first call was made ; he feared we might suffer for his help, but the good God he loved provided for us. It is three years this month (February, 1864). I think, since he was ' buried with Christ in baptism ;' but more than a year previous to that time he, with a few older Christians, had gathered a mission Sabbath-school in one of the most destitute suburbs of our city ; and from the time he first became interested in it, until his leaving with his regiment, I don't believe he had been absent more than three times. Most of the time he had more than two miles to walk, after attending church and the other Sabbath-school, of which he was Secretary and Librarian. Whatever. the weather might be, he would not be detained, saying, ' No ; if those poor children can come to be taught, I for one will be there to teach them.' The little beginning there made, has resulted in the most flourishing Sabbath-school in this city. After Charley had united himself with the church, he expressed a great desire that his father, who had long been a believer, but who was not connected with any church, should publicly put on Christ. He often conversed with me with regard to it, and before he left us, he himself begged him to do so. (Since his death that wish has been complied with.) He was an active Christian, always trying to be diligent in business, fervent in spirit, serving the Lord. When I was lamenting the step he had taken in leaving us for the war, he reproved me thus : ' Mother, where is your faith, am I not still in my Heavenly Father's hands ?' His letters, of which

I have many, are always cheerful, breathing a spirit of dependence on God, and of trusting faith in Him, a faith which sustained him to the last. Never, in those fine, precious days, I was permitted to watch beside his dying bed, did I hear one murmur from his lips. The first day I was there I asked him whether he did not now regret having gone into the army. The answer was prompt—'Never for a moment.' 'But,' said I, 'those cruel-wounds!' 'I am proud,' he answered, 'of having received them for my country.' I said, 'Charley, it has been a precious thought to me, that you had the Saviour to lean on in your trials.' 'Oh, dear mother,' he replied, 'how precious He has been to me! He has kept me in great temptations and trials, and I can trust in Him now!' He never admitted how much bodily suffering he was enduring until that last night of his life. Then, in great agony he clasped my hand. I said, 'Dear child, how you are suffering!' 'Yes, mother,' he replied, 'more than I can tell you.' The confession seemed to have been wrung from him, for a moment after he said, 'But I can bear it;' and you know he did bear it, bravely, too. His last farewell was almost cheerful: 'Dear mother, I am almost worn out now; I'm going home;' and I trust he rests at home now where we shall shortly meet him."

One more extract, and the picture of the character of Charles Crary will be complete, as far as the letters in my possession can make it so. Mr. Clegg, the companion of Charles Crary, who had come with him to the Turner's Lane Hospital, strove day and night to relieve the sufferings of his comrade. "If I lose him," he said to me, "I lose my best earthly friend." But there was also not wanting, by the sick bed of young Crary, the sympathy of women, supplying, as far as possible, the absence of a mother or a sister's love, fanning the heated brow, offering the cooling drink, or watching by the side of the sleeping sufferer—offices of Christian sympathy which, in this case, received in part their deserved reward, when the mother of Charles Crary arrived, and poured out the gratitude of a mother's heart for all the kindness which had been shown to her wounded boy. One of the ladies has kindly furnished me with the following:

"August 3d, the last day of Charley's life, was intensely hot. His earnest question, 'Is there *no* air coming in at the window?' was one hard to answer in the negative, and showed how painful the struggle for life had become. Indeed, it was only by constant hard fanning that he seemed able to breathe at all. At one time, a bystander said to one who was fanning him, 'Let me take your place—you must be tired.' Poor Charley said, 'I am tired;' and when a wish was expressed that he might be rested, he said, 'Oh, it don't matter much—it will be only a few days longer!' So few and so simple were the expressions which told us how much he was suffering. The touching words, 'Mother, I am almost worn out, I'm going home,' and a murmured—'Father!' were the last we heard; and, in a few moments, after a very brief struggle, he was at Home, in a land where the inhabitant shall no more say, 'I am sick,' and where the weary are at 'rest.' * * It was with gratitude that those who had been permitted to wait upon him acknowledge the privilege, and the emptiness of his place was felt when he was taken away. He rests now in Elanwood, a cemetery near his Western home."

Having thus availed myself of the knowledge which those who best knew Charles Crary were able to furnish, there is but little for me to add.

The last days of his life were like his letters home, or like those he dictated while in our hospital, full of hope, and abounding in expressions of gratitude to God. The hymns which we sang from evening to evening in our prayer meetings, and which he could overhear while lying on his bed, would recall to his mind similar scenes at his home in Detroit. The services of the sanctuary, the Sunday-school of which he had had charge, and the meetings for prayer in which he had taken a part, would pass in review upon his spiritual eye, and would call forth new strains of gratitude, on account of the comfort which these reminiscences afforded him. There is, however, one recollection which I would not willingly pass over in silence. At the very time that earthly ties of the most endearing character were breaking asunder, the bonds which defy death were shining forth in all their heavenly brightness. The mother took her darling boy from her bosom, where he had so often nestled, to lay him into the grave; but, while doing so, all that seemed dark below was lit up by that faith in the Lord Jesus Christ which filled both mother and son, and by the full assurance that shortly they would be united again, never to part.

The outline of the sermon which elder Chase preached at his funeral in Detroit, from Heb. xi., 4. well sums up what the pages here presented exhibit somewhat in detail: "As a son, Charles was dutiful and affectionate; as a young man, virtuous, kind, energetic, persevering, modest; as a Christian, whole-souled, faithful, earnest, diligent in duty; as a patriot and a soldier, always ready and courageous; he gave his life for his country, 'He being dead, yet speaketh.'"

A few remarks of a general character, and I have done. The spiritual life of Charles Crary has its counterpart in every part of the country, and in every relation of life. Of this fact I receive new proofs from day to day. There are those who, in our own hospital, have become interested in the great question of their soul's salvation, or with whom for a time I have enjoyed spiritual fellowship, and who are now at their homes, or in the front, facing and fighting the enemy. Their letters to me plainly show that they are still endeavoring to fight faithfully the great spiritual battle in which they have engaged. Others, again, who have lost with us those whom they most dearly loved, have learnt to feel that even by such great bereavements, the Lord has brought them nearer to himself. On these facts it is almost useless to dwell. The cases where the power of God's Spirit has been manifested are to be met everywhere. There are those who, in spite of these facts, are shrugging their shoulders, thinking that no permanent good is to be expected from any such temporary excitements, and yet how strange it would be if it were otherwise. When a child, I lived in the midst of events not unlike those of the present day. The Prussian monarchy had been crushed by Napoleon; Queen Louisa had died broken-hearted; and dying, had asked her sons, one of whom is now King of Prussia, to die for their country, if they could not live for it. But then, Prussia humbled herself before the Lord, and going forth with new energy, contributed very substantially to the overthrow of Napoleon. Such were the effects which the judgments of God produced in the case of Prussia; and would it not be strange if, in our case, these judgments would be altogether in vain? But they are not in vain. In many an hospital, in many a camp, on many a battle-field, in many a dreary prison, in many a bereaved home, and on many a lonely mountain side, the spirit of God is quickening the hearts of men, and is drawing them to himself. It is a knowledge of this fact which fills me with new hope, when I am tempted to look away from God and to feel discouraged, because there is still so much vice prevailing. The leaven is at work, and the time may yet come when the kingdom of heaven, little indeed in its beginnings, shall be like the tree, in the branches of which the birds of the air rejoice to dwell.

I will join hand in hand with the advocate of temperance; my ear and my heart shall be open in behalf of the enslaved; I will engage in every effort which shall advance the intelligence of the people; but never shall I suffer myself to be carried away by the popular idea, that by such efforts the prosperity and the happiness of the people is to be permanently secured. To secure them, a far deeper foundation is needed. What would you think of a man attempting to dam up a stream while the fountain was left to pour forth its abundant waters? As little can you secure the happiness of a people as long as you leave the fountain of evil untouched. The sin which lies at the root of all our troubles, is that we have not believed in the Son of God. The Spirit has come to testify of Him, and we have not heeded the voice of the Spirit. The God-man has come, and has desired to be enthroned in our hearts, and we have not admitted him. If we, as a nation, persist in this spirit, neither success on the battle-field, nor zeal for the emancipation of the enslaved, nor the removal of any other crying sin, nor the spread of intelligence by the means of public instruction, can furnish the needed remedy. Out of the heart are the issues of life! In the same measure as I see the head of the nation turn in contrition to God, I feel comforted: and thankful.

indeed, am I, to know that the soldier to whose brief life these pages have been devoted, and who not only has fought for his earthly country, but who has also fought the good fight of faith, is but one out of a great and noble army. Through much tribulation they have entered and are entering the kingdom of heaven.

But to conclude. I have at all times felt it to be both an honor and a joy to be a citizen of this country, but never have I felt more strongly that this is my true home, than since these calamities have come upon us; and since I have been enabled from day to day to scatter seed, which, with the blessing of God, may contribute in some measure to the way for a firmer trust in God, and for a more living faith in the Lord Jesus Christ. May the blessing of God continue to rest upon the many efforts which are now made to advance His cause.

THE TURNER'S LANE HOSPITAL.

THE TURNER'S LANE HOSPITAL.

To prepare the reader for what I have to say with regard to the Turner's Lane Hospital, I beg leave to submit to him a few remarks concerning the Army of the United States. I do not mean to address the soldiers of that army in the voice of flattery; it is heard but too often and by no means commends to their hearers those who employ it. I do not wish to conceal the fact, that a portion of that army consists of those who have entered it simply because they obtain a certain amount of bounty, or from other considerations of a like character; nor am I disposed to forget that I have met with those who preferred to walk crooked though their spine was not injured, and with some who by other devices attempted to escape from active service. I shall not attempt to give the impression, that the soldiers of the United States are men who are every way superior to the great mass of citizens, and whom I can hardly meet without feeling disposed to take off my hat. If I were to make such an effort I would get but poor thanks from those whose approval is of value, and for their sakes as well as my own, I shall abstain from it.

What I meant to say is, that with all the deductions it may be necessary to make, there yet remains the fact that in the same measure as we submit the principles of action by which the great majority of the Army of the United States are influenced, to a careful examination, we are filled with the conviction that in many respects they occupy a position altogether peculiar in the history of the world. It is not only the determination to preserve unimpaired the national existence, and to rest not till the rebellion is crushed, which impels them to action; the Emperor of China has struggled for a similar end. In the soul of the American soldier there is at the same time the consciousness that he is

(61)

fighting for the cause of freedom, and his arm is nerved by the thought that as he is to maintain the free institutions of his country, so is his country to favor the cause of freedom throughout the universe. And this feeling is not to be thought lightly of, as the effect of national vanity. Slowly and silently perhaps, but on that account not less surely and effectually, has the peaceful progress of America tended to lighten the weight of oppression and to prepare the way for constitutional freedom in other parts of the world, and in consequence of it, millions have left their homes in Europe to join in sustaining the institutions which had been the means of securing such general prosperity. Appreciating the benefits which they confer, it is not astonishing that when it had become evident that it was by an appeal to the sword alone that the overthrow of these institutions could be prevented, thousands of them should be found ready to enter the ranks of the Army of the United States.

But there is a still deeper current of feeling in the hearts of many of the American soldiers which invites our attention. The peculiar influences under which this country has been settled, have never altogether lost their force. It is a faith handed down from father to child that this country is to be the means of spiritual blessings to the world, and the pious soldier sees in the changes which every day almost is ushering in, an evidence of the presence of God who is thus preparing the people of the United States to become better fitted for the part they are to take in the conversion of the world. With one* who has ably developed the thought that our country is to be the chief national instrumentality in the reformation of christendom and the conversion of the world, I would ask, when there was ever such a prayerful going forth to battle in the holy and cheerful spirit of christian sacrifice? European officers high in command have paid a frank tribute to the superiority of the Army of the United States, because the men who compose it are not only

---

* Influence of the United States on Christendom, a sermon delivered by Thomas H. Stockton, at the Church of the New Testament, Philadelphia, November 29th.

brave, but also remarkable for intelligence and for their being fully conscious of the high aims which they struggle to attain. The means I enjoy from day to day of watching the self-denying spirit of these men, give me ample opportunity to know that the praise thus freely given is not undeserved.

Having made these remarks by way of introduction, I am ready to invite my reader to enter with me the grounds of the Turner's Lane Hospital.

This Hospital is situated in the northwestern part of the City of Philadelphia, at a distance of about half a mile from Girard College. By the older inhabitants the situation is remembered as a country residence, the inmates of which, for many years, bore a part in whatever of joy or sorrow might visit the neighborhood in which they lived. In the course of time the property passed into the hands of an association of Germans, who devoted it to hospital purposes. In the year 1862, this association rented it to the Government of the United States, and on the 13th of August of that year it was opened for the reception of soldiers. In addition to the main building which is principally used for officers, and a smaller building which the ladies interested in the Hospital occupy, the Government has constructed a number of barracks. The place has not, however, altogether lost its rural appearance since the space which is encircled by these barracks is still covered with the trees and the shrubbery of former days, while the well-cared for green house shelters the flowers which in the spring shall again gladden the inmates of the Hospital.

Another part of the grounds is occupied by the kitchen, the library, the dispensary, and such smaller buildings as the business of the hospital requires.

Dr. R. A. Christian, Surgeon U. S. V., the present head of the hospital, has been in charge of it since June 15th, 1864.

The gentlemen who have preceded him are:

Dr. G. Wood, in charge from August 13th, 1862, to September 18th, 1862.

Assistant Surgeon E. S. Dunster, U. S. A., in charge from September 18th, 1862, to March 12th, 1863.

Assistant Surgeon C. H. Alden, U. S. A., in charge from March 12th, 1863, to June 15th, 1864.

On the third of December, 1862, I succeeded the Rev. Robert Graham in the capacity of Chaplain of this hospital. As appears from the dates just given, during the greater portion of my service in this hospital, I have stood officially connected with Dr. Alden. As his position in this hospital now belongs to the memories of the past, I need not deprive myself of the pleasure of saying that he is remembered by many in this hospital with affection and regard.

Since the opening of the hospital, there have been admitted to it up to this date (Dec. 14th) 2,632 patients; of these, 1,173 have been returned to duty, 401 have been transferred to other hospitals, 281 have been discharged from service, and 49 have died. Since the 27th of September, this hospital has been more especially used for the treatment of nervous cases, which do not often put a sudden period to life; to this fact may be in part ascribed the small number of deaths, as above recorded; it is principally due, however, to the skill of the operator, and to the faithfulness with which the progress of disease has been watched, as well as to the physical, intellectual and spiritual influences which contribute to the recovery of health, with which this hospital has been favored.

The remarks I have to offer, with regard to the Turner's Lane Hospital, will have reference principally to its spiritual life—since, as the chaplain of the hospital, that portion of its history has been brought more especially under my notice. Yet, before entering upon this task, I cannot but say that the worldly interests of the hospital are so ably attended to, that I cannot but devote to them a passing notice.

The hospital is under the management of a Steward, who is conscientious in the disposition of the funds entrusted to him, a fact which deserves to be noted, as there have been stewards who have been wanting in this respect;—who is so judicious in his purchases that, in a city which numbers not less than 600,000 inhabitants, where there is so much competition, and where it is so difficult to. achieve eminence, he has acquired the reputation of being one of the best caterers, and who is ever ready to minister to the spirits as well as the bodies of the soldiers, by making the strains of music and the voice of song contribute to their entertainment.

It is but justice to say, that whatever reputation this hospital has for efficiency, it owes in a goodly degree to the intelligent zeal of B. F. Spafford, Hospital Steward, U. S. A.

Hospital life, in all its phases, since the beginning of the war, has occupied so many able pens, that the great mass of the reading public are likely to be sufficiently well informed with regard to it. They know that the spiritual life of hospitals is subject to peculiar influences; that from each important battle-field numbers of wounded men are sent to them; that the dangers through which these men have passed often fill them with serious thoughts, and that as the varying scenes of the march and the excitement of battle are exchanged for the quiet and the retirement of the hospital. their hearts and minds, with a feeling of more than usual tenderness, turn to the loved ones at home, or to the better home in heaven; they also know, or they will easily infer, that under such circumstances, a kind word from the chaplain, or from some kind-hearted visitor, is likely to meet with a ready response, and that therefore a chaplain's congregation is not without many elements of peculiar interest.

There is no need then to dwell on the encouragement which the chaplain derives, when, at the hour of preaching, he sees himself surrounded by a congregation many of whom are hanging upon his lips with strange intenseness, since perchance, for months past they have not heard the Gospel, and others, because the scenes through which they have passed have given them a new power of understanding it; nor shall I attempt to enter into particulars with regard to the meetings for prayer, where bands of brothers meet and part, not to meet again in most cases till the Great Day of Account. There is indeed but one feature to which I shall call the reader's attention with regard to these prayer meetings. When there has been a good deal of fighting going on, these accessions are of course of frequent occurrence, and, as at times, soldiers come to our hospital who in a day or two may leave it for some other, liberty is given to all to speak or to pray as the Spirit may prompt. When on such occasions, with the confession of sin and a deep sense of the reality of a Judgment to come, there is heard mingling evermore the expression of adoration and of endearment with regard to Him who had come to honor the law and to die "for us," who has become "the propitiation for our sins," and "through whose stripes we are healed;" the High Priest who can feel for our infirmities, and who is at the same time powerful to deliver us from them, and who has proved himself most near in the hour of greatest need, the mind of the listener instinctively turns back to the conflicts through which, age after age the church has passed in defending the Truth she holds, and derives new confidence and hope from the united confession of these little bands of believers. The missionaries, laboring in foreign lands, tell us that when at rare intervals they meet with brother missionaries, the consciousness of their being one in Christ, partakers of the same Divine life, throws into shade every question of denominational differences. There is in the spiritual life of the hospital something similar to this. It will hardly be thought strange that even when in one instance, a German brother forgetting that he could not be understood, poured forth his confession and his petitions in his native tongue, it did not interrupt this consciousness of being one in Christ, but made it rather more deeply felt.

What I have said with regard to hospital life in general applies also to the labors in which many christian woman have engaged in connection with them. While they have gone forth unobtrusively, prompted by patriotic and christian principles, in order to alleviate suffering, their self-denying and persevering labors have not failed to call forth the praise they deserve. It is therefore rather to satisfy my own heart than to convey information, that I say of the ladies connected with the Turner's Lane Hospital, that the attention they have paid to those who need articles of food which the Government does not furnish, the interest they have manifested in the wives and the children of the soldiers, their efforts for their instruction and their amusement, and the gentleness and affection with which they have endeavoured to arouse the spiritual life of the inmates of the hospital are gratefully remembered, not only by many of those who are yet members of it, but also by many others who have left it but with whom I am still in correspondence. I feel thankful, indeed, that my intercourse with them does not only belong to the memories of the past, but that it is my daily privilege to enjoy their counsel or to join with them in labors of love.*

One of them, however, is no longer with us. Mrs. Elizabeth Abbott, the lady-matron of this hospital, from the time it was first opened, departed this life while I was on a distant field of duty. In her case, as in the case of every faithful christian, we have reason to rejoice that her comparatively short stay amongst us is full of pleasant memories.

Favored by the possession of a large fortune, the ardent devotion of a husband and the warm affection of a large circle of relations and friends, her life for many years seems to have flowed on so smoothly that the preparation for eternity which we all need seems to have been lost out of sight. The long protracted sickness by which her husband was afflicted till death brought relief, was the means of gradually withdrawing her from the gaieties of society and of leading her to more serious thoughts. The shock which the death of Mr. Abbott produced on her was so great that it seemed as if she would sink under it. At the same time, however, it became the means of convincing her that she needed a higher than human power to sustain her in her deep affliction. Her husband had been a member of the Orthodox branch of the Society of Friends. She now became a member of that organization, and in doing so, made no secret of the fact that the unsatisfactory character of all that is earthly had been revealed to her, and that she sought Him who is the Truth and the Life.

At the time when these spiritual yearnings had been

---

* The labors of Miss Otto and Miss Troutwine in connection with a Bible Class formed in the Turner's Lane Hospital, have been greatly blest, and have been often the means of drawing attention to cases of special interest. Miss Troutwine is still with us.

awakened in her, the Turner's Lane Hospital was opened in the immediate vicinity of her residence. She was invited to take an active part in alleviating the sufferings of the sick and the wounded. She accepted the invitation, and there is no doubt that in the same measure as she endeavored to impart comfort to others, her own spirit was comforted. From the time of the opening of this hospital, in the summer of 1862, she continued to preside over the counsels and the efforts of the circle of ladies connected with it, till she was prevented by her sickness, in the month of August, 1864. On her death-bed, her only trust was "Christ, the blessed Son of God." Her life of faithful devotion to duty, while connected with this hospital, has been in beautiful harmony with this confession. The ladies who for so long a time have been associated with her in labors of love, and the officers and surgeons who have been brought in contact with her on many occasions of official or social intercourse, will bear me out in the tribute which I am thus offering to her memory. The soldiers who have experienced the care with which she watched over their bodily comfort, and the earnestness with which she supplied whatever might contribute to their spiritual welfare, will never forget her. When, in the letters which I receive from those who have left the hospital, mention is made of the kindness they have experienced at the hands of the ladies connected with this hospital, the name of Mrs. Abbott always occupies a prominent place.

I have only to add, that my intercourse with Mrs. Abbott has left on my mind the impression of one who was remarkable, not only for a cultivated literary taste and a highly genial spirit, but also for deep humility and an earnest desire to know and to do her duty.

The glance which I have cast at the spiritual life of the inmates of the Turner's Lane Hospital, suggests a brief reference to the manner in which God is likely to overrule our national trials for our good.

Trench, in his lecture on the "Progressive unfolding of Scripture," speaks of it as a Book intended for the education of man, since it contains the gradual unfolding of a thought which could have only entered into the mind of God to con-

ceive, and which He only, who is the King of everlasting
ages, could have carried out. In developing this idea, he
dwells on the different epochs in the national life of Israel:
on Abraham's child-like faith, on the sense of alienation from
God, awakened by the giving of the law and of the meeting
in Christ of Righteousness and Love. There are similar
epochs in the history of every nation, and ours is in the act
of giving a striking proof of it. With the beginning of the
struggle in which we are now engaged, we have been leaving
the age, when, with child-like confidence, we persuaded ourselves that all was well. Being now delivered up to the
stern discipline of the law, it may aptly be said, that we are
engaged in a wilderness journey, which is to prepare us for
a better future. If I were to say that this better future
which God intends for us is to be obtained, not by the casting off of this or that national sin, but by faith in the Son of
God, that it is of this that the spirit of God has come to con-
vince the world, and that it is to draw to Him that the
Father is constantly casting out his cords of love, the words
might fall strangely upon the ears of some, and yet it is by
our nearness to Him that nations as well as individuals shall
be judged, and it is our nearness to Him which is highest
bliss. The readiness with which men and women, favored
by position and fortune in many instances, seek for lasting
joy in caring for those who are less favored; the thought
that God is in the overturnings which our country is experi-
encing, and a willingness to submit to his righteous judgment which we meet frequently and in quarters where we
least expected it, and that divine charity which many sad
provocations have caused only to shine more brightly, and
of which the actions as well as the sayings of our President
present a noble example; all these are indications that the
purifying process to which we are now subjected is producing some cheering results. It also deserves attention that
many organizations which the necessities of our time have
called into existence, are in a great degree pervaded by a
spirit which belongs not to this earth alone, though the
inquiry may be instituted, whether, in our public philan-
thropic labors, there is not room for our acting more from

principle than from excitement and, unconsciously, perhaps, from a willingness to fall in with what happens to be popular.* It is also more than probable that, as individuals, we are at times forgetful that, as Trench beautifully expresses it, "it is when we are welcoming and fulfilling the lowliest duties which meet us in the common paths of a christian life, we shall often be surprised that we have unawares been welcoming and entertaining angels."

Among the topics which are intimately connected with the welfare of our soldiers, is the care which some of their families stand in need of. I am not astonished that the pastors of this city find their feelings, their time, and their labors enlisted in the families of soldiers, who, from various reasons, are suffering. The ladies connected with the Turner's Lane Hospital, as well as myself, are called from day to day to engage in similar efforts. Whether these sufferings arise from guilt or neglect, or whether they are occasioned by circumstances over which the Government can have no control, are not subjects which call for a consideration on the present occasion. . I know that I have to devote myself to this work, and that I have to enlist the help of others as far as I may.

A second topic to which I wish to direct the attention of the reader, is the care which the orphans of those need, who have fallen on the field of battle. I have become somewhat intimately acquainted with one of the institutions intended in part, at least, to meet this want. A brief history of it may be the means of enlisting the reader's interest in other institutions of a similar character.

When in 1862, I arrived in this city, after having made my escape from the Southern Confederacy, I learned that a clergyman, the Rev. E. Bœhringer, who had labored as a missionary in the cities of Norfolk and Richmond, had also

---

* It was probably a train of thought, such as I now am indulging in, which has led a member of the debating society in Turner's Lane Hospital to maintain the other day that, while our feelings are justly enlisted in the cause of the colored people, we are too forgetful of what we owe to the Cherokees, whose loyalty and whose sufferings may well be placed by the side of East Tennessee.

succeeded in escaping. I of course felt an interest in making his acquaintance, but for more than a year after did not meet him again. Then, however, I learned that he had started an Orphan Asylum, and that he intended to pay especial attention to the orphans of soldiers. Meeting him in the month of August, I promised him that as soon as I should return from a journey I was then about to undertake, I would join him in making an effort to increase the funds of the Institution. After an absence of two months I returned to this city, and learned that the Rev. E. Bœhringer and his wife had departed this life.

Fifty children had been received into the Asylum at the time of Mr. B.'s death. To these are now added the six children of the founder of the Institution. In the language of one who has lately visited the Institution and there met these children: "If it be, as we know it is, one of God's favorite attributes to care for the fatherless under all circumstances, we cannot doubt but that orphans, who have been made such in the service of the orphan cause itself, must have a more than common claim on His regard; and *their* presence in an Orphans' Home may well be taken, therefore, as the surest token it can have of His continual favor and blessing."

This Orphans' Home is under the regular supervision of the Board of Directors for Orphans' Homes, appointed by the General Synod of the German Reformed Church, and under the immediate management of a Committee of Ministers and Laymen of that body.

The Committee have purchased a suitable piece of property at Bridesburg, and are making additions to it, which are greatly needed. To defray the expenses, a subscription list has been started, on which the names of many prominent citizens are already found. If the Lord should move the hearts of any to do something for these orphans, the letter containing the contribution should be addressed to the present head of the Institution, the Rev. J. Gautenbein, Orphans' Home, Bridesburg, Philadelphia, Pa.

The third topic to which I wish to refer, is the attention which those need who have been disabled by the loss of limbs or other severe injury. The opening of the Christian Street Hospital for purposes of this kind, promises to meet this want in a great measure. It is my earnest prayer that the Surgeon in charge and the Chaplain of that hospital may be abundantly sustained by the patriotic and benevolent in our community. I do not know a class of men in many of whom I feel a deeper interest than these maimed soldiers.

The fourth and last topic which calls for some reference on my part, is the attention which is due to the German soldiers of our army. From the time when (thirty-seven years ago) I came to this country to the present day, I have held that every proper step should be taken which may serve to .remove the barriers which a difference of language is likely to keep up between different portions of our popula-'lation. Still there are cases when the means of grace should be provided for them. I am thankful that the Christian Commission is employing a German missionary to visit the German soldiers in our hospitals. The enterprize of the Rev. Mr. Romich, who has been the means of erecting a church edifice at the corner of Poplar and Twenty-first streets, also commends itself to every one who is aware how important it is that our German emigrants should be provided with the means of grace.

In now bringing this article to a close, I am conscious that I have used but a small portion of the material at my disposal. These are the letters which, from time to time, have been addressed to me, or to the ladies interested in our hospital, by soldiers who were with us for a time. The very uncertainty whether these soldiers are still with Grant, with Sherman, or with Thomas, or whether they have gone to their final rest, give a solemn interest to the statements they contain; and there are the sketches of their experience since the commencement of the war, which several of the soldiers, by my request, have furnished me; and there is the diary, which I have kept, and which, imperfect as it is, contains accounts deserving of notice.

Nor have I said anything of the liberality with which the

Bible Society, the Tract Society, and the Christian and Sanitary Commissions, have attended to the wants of the soldiers; or of the readiness with which the Army Committee of the Young Men's Christian Association has, from time time, made valuable additions to our library. My duties in the hospital leave me too little leisure to draw upon these stores, or to dwell upon the evidence this hospital has received of the great usefulness of these associations. And, in conclusion, I can only say, that I am deeply grateful for the manner in which I have been treated by all who, from time to time, have been connected with this Institution. They have borne with my weaknesses, they have overlooked my short-comings, and, as far as I know, they have never doubted that it is my earnest and prayerful desire that the cause of the Lord Jesus Christ may be established and built up in the hearts of those who are entrusted to my spiritual care. I trust that my future course shall be marked by increased faithfulness.